P9-AFJ-487

Hard Language

Hard Language

Short Stories

by

Mike Padilla

Arte Público Press
Houston, Texas

This volume, as first-place winner of the annual University of California-Irvine Chicano/Latino Literary Contest, is made possible through sponsorship of the Department of Spanish and Portugese, School of Humanities, University of California at Irvine.

Recovering the past, creating the future

Arte Público Press
University of Houston
Houston, Texas 77204-2174

Mike Padilla
  Hard language / by Mike Padilla.
    p.   cm.
  ISBN 1-55885-298-0 (pbk. : alk. paper)
  1. California — Social life and customs — Fiction. I. Title.
  PS3566.A3313 H37 2000
  813'.6—6dc21   00-041632
                                          CIP

♾ The paper used in this publication meets the requirements of the American National Standard for Information Sciences—Permanence of Paper for Printed Library Materials, ANSI Z39.48-1984.

Several of the stories in this collection have appeared elsewhere in different form: "Papel," in *Sequoia,* "The Reason for Angels," in *Indiana Review;* "Flora in Shadows," in *Puerto del Sol;* "Carrying Sergei," in *North Dakota Quarterly;* "Hard Language," in *The Americas Review;* and "Restoration," in *Kiosk.*

Library
University of Texas
at San Antonio

© 2000 by Mike Padilla
Printed in the United States of America

0 1 2 3 4 5 6 7 8 9   0 9 8 7 6 5 4 3 2 1

For Dave

Contents

Acknowledgments

The author gratefully acknowledges the support and encouragement of The San Francisco Foundation and Intersection for the Arts, the Department of Spanish and Portuguese at the University of California at Irvine, Michelle Carter, Tobias Wolff, George DeWitt, Mark Coggins, Terry Gamble, Monica Mapa, Suzanne Lewis, and Cassia Herman.

Hard Language

PAPEL

THE BIG JOKE *Tío* Henry always told my *tías* was that old Eufrasia's house would go up in flames just like her burnt *chicharrones*. All that frayed electrical wiring that hung from the ceiling was too expensive to replace, she'd told them, though the government had offered to fix all the electricity in her village in 1958. I was careful never to laugh too hard, and a look from my mother always told me when to stop. When Eufrasia's heart gave out for the fourth and last time, my *Tío* Uncle Henry and my *tías* drove south of the border as if a gun had gone off in a race. They came from Anaheim, from Glendale, from wherever they'd been waiting that late September morning.

On the bus from La Jolla my mother fidgeted with crochet needles, knitting a flowered pattern, unraveling it, knitting it again more tightly. She'd taken me out of school right when the first bio test was being passed out—the same test she'd locked me indoors to study for all week.

"When can I go back to school?" I stretched my legs and pressed my tennis shoes flat against the seat in front of me, flexing the calves that biking had begun to develop.

"Soon enough." She poked my leg with one of the hooks. She'd exploded into the classroom without asking the attendance office, had rushed past the biology teacher without looking at him, past the transparent anatomy model. "*Toma tus cosas, muchacho,*" she'd said. Some of the boys in back had snickered when she took my hand. "*Ándale, tu futuro te espera.*" If the words about the "future waiting for me" had been in English, the world might not have felt like it was slipping from under my feet as I ran after her down the waxed hallway.

Three days earlier, I'd met Jeremy and his friends at the reservoir on my bike. For the first time they hadn't spun off without me. They'd met me with a challenge, gripping their handlebars to intimidate me, but I out-biked every one of them, except Jeremy. For the rest of the week I'd spent lunch with them instead of eating alone. I'd started food fights, cornered girls in the hallway so they'd be late for classes, and gotten dragged into the principal's office twice. Even fat Charlie couldn't get into their group, and he was a fat white boy who

1

got new rims and bearings when it wasn't even his birthday or Christmas. *Tío* Henry had been right: it's physical strength that gets people's respect.

"When we buy the new house, we'll have a swimming pool," I said, as if there were no question about it.

She pulled some yarn from her bag and nodded.

"And a pool table. Then I can invite the guys over on weekends."

"Tell me again what you will say if *Señora* Johnson asks."

"That my father called," I said. "That he invited us over for the weekend."

"Where?"

"Newport Beach. Wherever that is. What am I going to tell the guys in class?"

"Say nothing. And don't let them influence you, *mu-cha-cho*," she said, pointing the hook at me with each syllable. "You're much too young for their bad ways. Keep to your school work so you. . . ."

"So I can make something of myself." I'd heard it all before—the education, the money, the better life. What good was it if I had to live it alone, like my mother did, with only her knitting baskets and Bullocks catalogs for company?

"Can I call Jeremy tonight? If he thinks I've blown him off, I won't stand a chance with the group." Being one of only three non-whites in school left my odds at about ten to one, I figured.

She leaned over me, face to the glass. The bus had stopped at the border, and outside two patrollers in brown uniforms talked to each other. One of them came inside the bus, surveying us from behind mirrored glasses. My mother's hands flitted from her lap to her hair to the collar of her dress.

"What are you so afraid of?" I said.

"It's hard to put the past behind you," she said. She meant before she could afford to live on the outskirts of La Jolla, before she was a legal citizen.

I slumped in my seat and watched the next ten minutes tick by on my watch. My mother had promised that now the past wouldn't matter, that we'd begin a whole new life. No more shopping out of town, or saving bottles for their deposits, or secondhand space heaters to pay the La Jolla rent. But other things she told me about made her work her dress collar even harder: electrolysis for her legs, new designer clothes, wall-to-wall carpeting, and a silver tea service to entertain her guests. I had no idea where they'd come from. As for me, I'd have a new dirt bike, and when I was old enough, my own car. A new La Jolla house seemed far in the future, but she promised it within a few months.

But for now my mind was on Tijuana. My mother said it was barren of opportunity, but this time it would yield something for me. On the streets they sold firecrackers, the kind any boy in school would pay fifty cents a pack for.

Driving into the village, I pressed my face against the glass. There were the same squat, box-like houses, the same bulky, twisted fig trees up and down the road. My fingers gripped the vinyl armrest.

"God," I said. "No telephone poles. *No phones!*"

❧ ❧ ❧

During the funeral the priest spoke too quickly for me to follow the Spanish. When it was over I took my feet down from the bench in front of me. My mother and I never went to the Presbyterian church she'd joined, but I knew it wouldn't have felt like this Tijuana chapel, with its burning incense and cold cement floor. The people moved slowly out the door.

"Quickly, quickly," she said, but only I could hear her.

The women on the porches of the low, flat-roofed houses stopped washing and chatting to give us sad looks. I tried to imagine my mother crouched over a washboard in one of her designer dresses that she had bought at the clearinghouse. But the picture wasn't even funny.

I stopped along the way to stamp the dust out of my shoes, but raised more, turning my ankles orange up to the knee. This road would be perfect for my dirt bike. I could see myself on my Bridgestone, head down, barreling into the wind, feet whipping around the crank, a long, thick stream of dust jetting out from beneath the back tire. Up the road, dry hills rose and dropped behind houses, showing off hollows, terraces, grooves, and steep inclines perfect for nose-diving and skidding. Even the rocky, pitted streets that never ran parallel invited good biking. If I could bring this home with me, I thought, instead of just firecrackers.

"It is like Tijuana not to have straight paths between places," *Tío* Henry said. I'd spotted him ducking through the chapel door five minutes before the service was over. "And look at their chickens on public display. An eyesore."

Short-haired mongrel dogs roamed the streets just as they had a year and a half ago, when old Eufrasia had fallen backwards in a chair just after my twelfth birthday. There had been fever, vomiting, and heart palpitations. The doctors had said she wouldn't live, but she pulled through with us at her bedside. She wasn't even my grandmother, but my mother's grandmother. She was deaf, distant, and very wrinkled, and she talked of things that seemed to have happened hundreds of years ago.

"Don't let the old woman upset you," my mother had told me when we were out of her room. "Hers is not a sharp mind like yours." She had proudly smoothed my black hair out of my eyes.

Still, though Eufrasia was deaf, no one ever said a disrespectful word in front of her, and not even the doctors touched her. And I can't remember, on any of our visits, that she ever put food to her lips or stirred a cup of coffee. She was like a spirit of the past that had chosen to remain in the world.

I walked a few paces ahead of my mother, *Tío* Henry, and *Tía* Margarita, so they'd know I was in a hurry to get this whole business over with. If I could get to a phone, I could call Jeremy. I'd tell him that the woman who'd yanked me from class was a maid, that she'd come to take me to the hospital because my mother had fallen down a flight of stairs. Maybe I could still go biking Sunday night at the reservoir.

"You'll have to tell these people to go away," *Tío* Henry said. "They're ignorant and must be told what to do."

"What difference will it make if Alicia is not there?" *Tía* Margarita said. She spoke in Spanish, as did all my aunts. "She is the only one who knows where to look." Margarita, the tallest and oldest of the sisters, walked with powerful, masculine steps, her head steady under the tall black hive of hair pierced with a metal comb. The matching beads looped around her neck chinked loudly with each step.

"Alicia is a strange one," *Tío* Henry said. "But she knows what will happen if she doesn't come. Now think of what you will say to these people."

A bus without windows came rattling around a blind corner as in a movie chase scene, lifting its left wheels a foot in the air. I dodged the cloud of orange dust it made.

"My clothes" *Tío* Henry said. "Damn this afflicted place." When I looked back, he was shaking a pebble from his shoe.

My mother slapped him hard across the back of the neck. "It's just a little farther, *hombre.*"

"Speak to me in English, woman," he said. He was a dark, short man with tight muscles that twitched in his neck when he spoke. "How can I find an American wife with everyone always speaking Spanish?"

"Look around you, *viejo estúpido.* Do you see any American brides blushing in these streets?" She tried to slap him again, but he was too quick for her. He grabbed her wrist so that she shrieked.

"*Hijo,*" my mother said. I looked back, but kept walking.

Margarita stepped in front of them, threatening *Tío* Henry with the iron heel of her shoe. "Stop this nonsense." Because the street was too rocky for heels, she went barefoot, one pump clutched in each hand.

"Maybe soon I can buy an American wife," he said, laughing.

"Yes," my mother said, turning her wrist slowly in her hand. "Soon we will all have what we want."

❧ ❧ ❧

When we reached the porch of Eufrasia's three-room house, Margarita punched one foot in each pump and mounted the sloping steps. Even if she hadn't stood at the top step, everyone in the crowd would have seen her high broad shoulders, her glossy mound of hair. She turned towards them, looking over them with her copper-green eyes. My mother, *Tío* Henry, and I went up the steps after her.

I recognized some relatives from across the border by their American clothes, but most of the people looked very poor. One man with a clean shave and neatly pressed pants smiled at me. I tried to eye him down, but he kept smiling, until I had to look away. I moved close behind *Tío* Henry.

Margarita folded her heavy arms, and for the first time I saw how her upper body resembled *Tío* Henry's. She looked as powerful as him, with similar deltoids and upper back size. No sport I could think of could have given them both that kind of form.

At last she said, "Go home and work, or pray for your souls. You have no business here." They walked away, their feet crunching in the dirt.

"What do they want?" I said.

"They don't want anything. They only adored her." *Tía* Alicia stood in the doorway behind me. She led us into the bare front room of the house and lit the gas lantern. The yellow light flickered faintly against the wall.

She gathered her hair into a slick cord that fell almost to her waist. She was much shorter than her sisters, and so frail in the arms that she wouldn't have been good even at badminton. Just throwing her hair back seemed to require a lot of effort.

"You don't know anything," *Tío* Henry said. "If you did, you wouldn't still be living on this side of the border."

"You think like an American tourist," she said.

"I think like an American because I am one."

"Stop this," Margarita said, ducking into the bedroom.

"Give your *Tía* Alicia a kiss, *muchacho*," my mother said, nudging me toward my aunt with her bony fingers. I kissed her cheek.

She said, "People have been stopping since three this morning. They come to the foot of the steps, but they do not knock. They try to peer in the windows, they loiter by the chicken coup. I keep the lights off and the blinds down."

Margarita emerged from the bedroom in a glittery, bright green dress. It looked cheap and fit tightly over her bulk.

"*Qué vestido tan hermosísimo*," my mother said. "Where did you buy it?"

Margarita gave her a long stare, then said to me, "There is a pickax in the tool shack." When I came back, everyone had gathered in a half circle facing the far wall. They looked like they might be posing for a portrait, only no one smiled.

Alicia pointed to the center of the wall and said, "There." She knew all the places to tap, for she had visited the woman weekly, bringing her groceries, clothes, and other things from the Zona Norte. Eufrasia would only have food from the open markets, and wouldn't accept anything that came from the stores downtown—"*los supermercados americanos.*"

I handed Margarita the heavy pickax, and she told me to stand back. No one moved. She spread her legs as wide as she could in her dress. She practiced swinging the pickax with ease, swinging it up and out from the wall. My mother clapped her hands together and said, "It is like the launching of a ship," but no one looked at her.

The end of the pickax slid smoothly into the soft plaster. A piece gave way, crumbling white and powdery to the cement floor. She swung again and again; the mound of plaster grew as she cleared the opening. She leaned the pickax against the wall and pushed her hand through the hole. I stopped breathing, almost expecting it to come out deformed. When she withdrew her white, chalky hand, her large fingers clasped a roll of tightly wound bills. With her straight, white teeth she broke the string that held the roll together and let the bills unwind and peel away, falling to the floor in dull green curls. Tens, twenties, and fifties in American currency. She pulled out another roll. Then another, and another, like magic, reaching deeper into the wall each time.

"We are wasting time," she said, and we began to work. She handed me the pickax and I started to tear away the rest of the wall, stopping only now and then to catch my breath. Some of the rolls had come untied, leaving money in hard-to-reach places. My mother examined the junctures of the house's frame, while *Tío* Henry held the lantern up to the crevices where loose bills might have fallen. They worked together, taking turns holding the lantern. Once, when my mother found a bill that had tried to escape her, she snatched it out of the wall and said, "This will be your making, *muchacho.*"

Margarita watched from the doorway, legs astride, hefty arms folded over her bosom. I wondered why I was working and she wasn't. Her face remained rigid, deeply carved with lines that were black in the lantern light.

After nearly an hour *Tío* Henry took the pickax out of my hands. "Don't kill yourself," he said, and began to swing at what was left of the plaster.

The cabinets in the kitchen were nailed shut. *Tío* Henry pried them open with the chisel end of the pickax, swearing all the while. The nails shrieked with resistance, then popped loose. Preserve jars lined the shelves in neat rows. They were so tightly packed with money we had to pry the bills out with sewing scissors.

There was no thought of sleep now, with morning bringing the dull green bills to light. I gathered them up and started to count. My hands had turned gray, and I tried to wipe the dirt on my shorts. At first, I was slow at counting, but found that it was faster to separate the different denominations, then group them into stacks of five hundred each. I wrote on the floor with a piece of plaster to keep tally on the total.

With the scissors, my mother cut open the mattress along the seam that had been opened and resewn with black thread. She brought armfuls of bills out and piled them in front of me. As I smoothed out the twenties, I found some personal checks that had been written to Eufrasia and signed with X's.

Tío Henry patted my head and said, "You're doing well, you're good at mathematics. Physical strength gets you respect, but no one wants to marry an idiot." I turned the checks facedown on the floor.

"Yes, he is the best in his school," my mother said, though it wasn't true. "He has many friends because he is so smart."

Tío Henry laid his big hand on my shoulder and smiled down at me. "What would you like your uncle to buy you?"

"Firecrackers," I said, "for my friends at school."

He turned his face toward my mother. "Have you been sending this boy to Sunday school? This Christian generosity sends people like us to the poorhouse." He looked back at me. "Think of yourself for once."

"I want them for myself," I said.

"Ah, modesty is a weakness! Think of something else, Christian boy."

"Firecrackers," I said.

"Firecrackers are dangerous," my mother said.

"Think harder," *Tío* Henry said, holding up a fistful of green.

I felt the odds slipping. Twelve to one. Fifteen to one. "I want to call somebody."

"Harder," he said. His face began to wrinkle with laughter.

The blood was in my cheeks again. Margarita was watching me from the doorway. I saw myself eating lunch alone at the end of a cafeteria table. I could taste the cold lunchmeat going down my throat. "I just want to get to a phone," I said, as calmly as I could.

"The Christian boy has a weak imagination." He took up another handful of dollars. "This stuff is power, but you have to know how to use it." He put his hand on my shoulder again and squeezed gently. "You'll learn, you'll learn."

He went back to swinging the pickax. My mother stripped open the sofa and started pulling out the stuffing. Margarita was still watching me with her copper-green eyes, as if she were waiting to see me cry. I held it back as hard as I could.

Margarita said, "The boy should eat something. I will take him to the store for milk and pan dulce." She took my hand as if I were a child and led me outside.

"*Tu madre y tu tío,* they don't understand you. *Pobrecito.*" Her hand felt cold and dry, rock-hard with muscle. It was good to hold on to. "Forget about them, they are both idiots. Soon you will see how foolish they are."

"What are you talking about?" I said.

"Your mother is nothing, but she thinks she is something. Your uncle is nothing, but he thinks something of himself, now that he had his citizenship papers. Someday you will find that you are nothing. Maybe your children or your grandchildren will be something." We stopped outside the store. Without looking at me, she bent down and gave me a hard kiss on the cheek.

"What about you?" I said. "What makes you think you're something instead of nothing?"

"Did I say I was not nothing?"

"Then you're nothing just like the rest."

"*No importa, muchacho.* You want firecrackers, am I right? I can get them for you." I looked up at her, but the sun blinded me. "Leave the back door open this afternoon when no one is in the house. I will put them in the wall behind the sofa. Make sure your mother doesn't see them."

She pulled me into the store and bought me milk and *pan dulce.* Then she pressed a fifty-dollar bill into my hand and said, "Say nothing."

❧ ❧ ❧

Alicia dragged a suitcase out of the bedroom. In it were some tarnished picture frames, old china, and some dresses. She held one of them up. "An unsightly thing, isn't it? Still, it can be restored."

"You can keep the artifact," my mother said. "The neighbors would think I was a maid come to do the cleaning."

"Use your imagination," *Tío* Henry said. He sprinkled a handful of twenties over Alicia's head.

"I think the diary is in the closet," *Tía* Alicia said. "But I can't find the key."

"What do you want with the old woman's scribblings?"

"She has many things written about the old ranching days."

"I'm not interested in her *historias*."

"No one said you had to be. Maybe the boy will find it interesting."

"Don't go filling his head with ancient nonsense. He's an American. He has the future to look to, not the past."

"It is time," Margarita said. I knew what she meant.

My mother said, "I have a child, remember." She pulled me close to her side of the couch and wrapped her thin arms around my waist. "I know I can't demand anything, but . . ."

"Your husband sends you alimony. That's why you divorced him," *Tío* Henry said. "You're not so special."

"I only meant . . ."

"Don't forget what happens if the authorities find out. You won't get half of what you're getting now."

My mother's eyes filled with tears, which she tried to wipe away before they spilled over. I tried to ignore her, but she pressed her face against my arm. I felt the moisture seep through my sleeve and couldn't move away.

"You should have been an actress," *Tío* Henry said. "Your tears might have profited you better."

She wiped her nose on my sleeve like a baby. "I want what is best for my son, not to have to live like this." She looked around her to indicate the room.

"You are far from this," he said.

"I want him to be someone."

Still in English, *Tío* Henry sang, "Somewhere, in the sometime, with that someone, I'll be someone at last . . ." He sang as if he were the only one in the room to hear it.

"See how your uncle treats his own flesh and . . ." A roll of money hit her sharply in the side of the face. Green paper exploded everywhere. The blood pulsed in my arms. She loosened her hold on me. I sat down and started counting again. *Tío* Henry leaned back on the sofa as if he were on a cruise to Acapulco.

"You must be sure never to grow up to be like your *tío*," my mother said calmly. "You must get a good education, make money so you can be somebody."

Tío Henry jerked himself forward. "And I'm not somebody?"

"An old fool."

"Do you see me begging like a dog?"

I counted the money very loudly in my head. I saw him throw something at her. Two-fifty, two seventy-five. Someone screamed. I counted. My mother ran to the bedroom. More shouting. Three-fifty, four hundred. Louder. Louder.

I ran out of the room and into the kitchen, took my books and went out. The screen door slammed behind me.

On the back steps I opened the book, but could barely see through the tears. Pictures of brains and hearts were blurred into odd shapes. As I thumbed through the pages of the later chapters, not reading them, hardly glancing at the pictures, the grayness of my hands came off on the pages. My hands were gray down to the pores, under the nails, in the creases of my palms, in the ridges of my fingerprints.

❧ ❧ ❧

Alicia was stroking my hair. "Go back to sleep, *niño*. You need your rest." I sat up abruptly and she stopped. Her fingers were cold, but her firm voice soothed me.

"What are you reading?" she said. "Ah, biology. Show me."

The book fell open to the plastic anatomy pages. I pointed to the first page, a drawing of a skeleton with a wide grin and white, ghostly ribs. I wondered how long before old Eufrasia would look that way in her grave. I flipped the next page over. Now the skeleton had veins, now arteries. I kept turning the pages, adding muscles, organs, tissue, pink skin and hair, until the picture became that of a complete person, shining pink and naked. I wondered what such a man would call himself. I wondered where he came from.

"You study too hard for a boy," she said. "Your *mamá* pushes you too hard."

"No," I said. "I don't care about school anymore." I closed the soiled pages of the book tightly and dropped it with the other books on the bottom step. "I need to call somebody back home."

"If that will make you feel better, *pobrecito,* I will take you." She started to run her fingers through my hair again, but brushed the hair out of my eyes instead. "We will go this afternoon."

❧ ❧ ❧

When *Tío* Henry asked me to fetch some water, I went out and filled two buckets to the rim. I carried them in, trying to make it look easy. He set them to heat on the stove. Most of the houses had running water, but Eufrasia had refused to allow them to tamper with her house.

"Crazy old woman," *Tío* Henry said as he washed his face in the water.

At noon a short woman in pants knocked at the screen door. Margarita filled the doorframe. The woman spoke in the kind of slow, distinct Spanish I could understand. "I'm *Señora* López from next door," she said. "I wanted to offer whatever condolences I could." Margarita didn't invite her in. Finally, the woman said, "It's my daughter's birthday. You're welcome to come by for coffee and cake, if you have the time."

"Thank you," Margarita said. "We will be by for a visit."

Alicia was in the kitchen. "It would be nice if we brought a gift for the girl," she said.

"Remember our birthdays as children?" *Tío* Henry said to my mother.

She turned away and said nothing. The roll of money had left a blue mark by her eye.

"Don't be angry with me," he said.

"A decent meal and a good bath is how we celebrated," she said, without turning. "And if one of us got a gift, we always broke it fighting over it. Why must you mention it?"

"I don't know," he said. "There's no reason to fight now, is there?"

She sat down and massaged her forehead. "I know. A better life."

He went out to the back yard and came back a few minutes later with two handfuls of eggs. "The birthday girl, her family is poor. She'll appreciate anything we can give them."

She straightened her back slowly, then looked at him. "It's a lovely gesture. Be sure they are the freshest ones."

Alicia turned away from them. "I will go to the Zona Norte and see what I can find." My mother and *Tío* Henry said nothing. Alicia looked at me. "Would you like to escort me on the bus?"

"Don't go depressing him with stories about the Old Town," *Tío* Henry said.

"Make sure he doesn't buy any *cuetes*," my mother said. "He'll blow his fingers off and not be able to hold a pencil."

"Keep your hands on your wallet," *Tío* Henry said.

✿ ✿ ✿

In all the commotion of the *mercado,* I couldn't find anyone selling fire-crackers. I had to be sure they would be here when Margarita came to buy them. I would tell her to bargain for six bricks and try to get some free bottle rockets in the deal. The people in the streets and produce stands shouted above the music of the mariachis—conversing, bargaining, advertising their goods to passersby. But nowhere did I hear the shouts of "¡*Cuetes*!" as I had last time.

Cars blew their horns to clear the streets of people. I walked fast in front of Alicia.

She grabbed me by the shoulder. "How do you expect me to keep up with you, *muchacho*?"

I saw a man waving a red package over his head walking toward us.

"Now what would a girl like for her birthday?" she said.

He got closer, but I lost him in the crowd.

"I always loved candy when I was a girl."

I spotted him again. He shouted in English, "Firecrackers! Firecrackers, cheap!"

"Don't get any funny ideas," she said. "Your mother will only take them away from you."

I looked over my shoulder as we walked past. He disappeared into the bright colors of the market. I checked the corner street sign. Madero and Seventh.

"Do you know who once stayed in that hotel over there? El Palacio, the pink one."

"*Tío* said not to tell me about the old days."

"*Ay*, do you think I care one way or the other what your *tío estúpido* thinks? That's where the American fighter Dempsey stayed."

"Jack Dempsey," I said, straining to be heard over the market noise.

"He fought your *Abuelo* Lupe in the twenties. All the men in the family went to see your grandfather almost lose the fight in the first round, but come back with a knockout punch in the third. Not many men have done that."

"I don't believe it," I said. But Jeremy would if I could make him. "My mother would have told me that."

"Your *abuela's* diary has the pictures of the fight in it."

"Did they have cameras back in the twenties?"

"You are making fun of me," she said. She walked ahead of me, but I caught up with her.

I couldn't hear the man with the firecrackers anymore. I tried to figure my odds again—somewhere between twenty to one and fifty to one, if Margarita got me the firecrackers. The noise in the market made it hard to think.

At the bus stop we couldn't sit down. There were too many people with souvenirs on the benches.

"What will the diary tell us?" I said.

"Everything."

Everything. How much longer was I going to have to wait for this slow bus?

"I'm going to buy firecrackers," I said. "I don't care what my mother says." I turned to run back into the crowd, but Alicia grabbed my arm.

"Your mother will cut my throat, *niño!*"

"Then, can I make my call now?"

She hesitated, then took out a handful of coins from her pocketbook.

Under an awning, a man in a print shirt was dialing a number over and over again. I clutched the change, jangled it loudly, kicked at the dirt. "No one's answering," I said to him.

"*Muchacho malcriado,*" he said, hanging up.

I dialed the operator. "Person to person. La Jolla, Estados Unidos."

"*Momento . . . diga.*"

I gave her Jeremy's name, then the number, half in Spanish, half in English. She said something too fast for me to understand.

"The bus is here!" Alicia was waving her arms at me.

I shoved more coins into the slot until the operator stopped talking. I'm at the hospital, I thought. My mother has fractured her collarbone in two places. If these operators talked slower, I could understand them.

One ring.

"*Está sonando.*"

A second ring.

I hung up before it could ring a third time.

On the bus I leaned my head against the window. My faint reflection disappeared in the sun, reappeared in the shade.

"Is it true that we're nothing?" I said.

"Ah." She nudged me in the ribs with her elbow. "Those are questions for the educated. Don't ask me about philosophy."

I watched the Old Town fall behind in the orange haze. "The diary will tell about the fight?"

"With pictures signed by both fighters."

"Can I keep them? My friends won't believe me. I was supposed to bring firecrackers, but this would be better."

She put her hand on my knee. I was glad *Tío* Henry was not there to see it. He would have called it a spectacle.

When we got back to Eufrasia's house, Margarita had put the money in the suitcase. I tried to lift it, but couldn't even slide it across the floor. I believed we'd never get it out the door, and the thought of a new life became just as unlikely. Margarita told me to close the back door. I stepped through the kitchen and slammed the door shut. Then I opened it quickly, just a crack.

✿✿ ✿✿ ✿✿

We found *Señora* López helping the children play pin-the-tail-on-the-donkey. When she saw us, she gestured for us to join her by the fire.

"Who is the birthday girl?" my mother asked

"Imelda, *la bonita* in the yellow dress," she said

"Yes, she is very pretty."

Tío Henry slumped in his chair, large fingers clasped around the mug between his legs. He stared into the fire. My mother stretched her legs under the table and kicked him. He sloshed beer into his lap, looked at Alicia, and sat up straight. Margarita sat a few feet away from the table, her arms folded.

Señora López brought out coffee and cookies on a tray. Only my mother took coffee.

"Have you lived here long?" she asked.

"Yes, I knew Eufrasia well. And were you close?"

My mother stirred her coffee briskly. "We tried to keep in touch. We were out for a visit a year and a half ago."

The shouts of the children filled the next few minutes. I'd thought that knowing Eufrasia would have been enough to start us talking. I hoped *Señora* López would tell about *Abuelo* Lupe, but no one mentioned him.

"It is a shame we didn't know her well," my mother said.

"She wasn't an easy woman to get to know."

"I must go," Margarita said. We watched her take long, pounding steps toward the street, her green dress glimmering in the last of the sunlight.

"She fought hard to save the school so the children wouldn't have to bus to town. Not even the government crossed her."

"She was important to the district," Alicia said. "She knew it and wasn't modest about it."

My mother sipped her coffee and *Tío* Henry said nothing.

"Why was she important?" I said. My mother tried to pinch me under the table, but I squirmed out of her reach. My heart beat faster. I thought, let's see what else you've kept from me.

"You see how the houses sit in bunches throughout the town?" *Señora* López said. "That is where the ranch hands lived. When ranching died, many of those people needed help to keep from starving."

"And *Abuela* gave them money?" I watched my mother's hands.

"She helped with food and laundry and children. The children hated her because she was so strict."

"Why did the tourists start coming?" I said.

"You have such a pretty girl," my mother said. "Such lovely hair."

"Because of the San Diego Exposition in 1915. They came by steam dummy."

"Steam dummy?"

"*Hijo*," my mother said. "Do not bother the *señora*. It is his schooling. They teach him to ask too many questions."

"A kind of boat?" I said.

My mother grabbed me, digging her fingers into my arm. I decided not to ask anything else. *Señora* López looked at her with wide eyes, and Alicia blushed.

"Thank you for everything," Alicia said, "but I'm afraid I must go."

Señora López got up to refill my mother's cup. *Tío* Henry said he would take some tequila if she had any. My mother watched her go into the house, then turned to the fire. Her face flickered with red light and shadows.

"She has many tales, doesn't she? She seems quite happy."

"She is too ignorant to see her condition clearly," *Tío* Henry said.

My mother smoothed out her collar. "We were lucky?"

"Lucky our parents escaped Tijuana before they died."

She folded her arms against the cold and gave him a long stare. "I was only thinking of the lies I tell the neighbors." She looked at him as if he were the cause of every bad thing that had ever happened to her.

An older child blindfolded the birthday girl and put a sawed-off broom handle in her hands. *Tío* drank the last drops of beer from the mug and placed it firmly on the table.

Señora López set a bottle and a glass in front of *Tío* Henry. The children had gathered around the piñata. One child bobbed it by yanking on the clothesline it was hanging from. The girl swung at the air, grazing the burro. *Tío* Henry drank shots quickly, refilling the glass every few minutes.

The piñata broke with a crack, and the children scrambled in the gravel. I remembered the *dulces de leche* Alicia had left for the girl and handed them to *Señora* López.

"We must go," *Tío* Henry said. He stumbled as he got up, tucking his shirt in at the back of his pants. His drooping eyelids shot open as he heard one of the children scream. Two girls were fighting for one of the prizes. His skin flushed in the firelight. "Margarita." He ran out of the yard, falling once, scrambling, rising again. *Señora* López went over to the children.

"The old fool," my mother said. "Too much tequila. Go after him."

I found him in the front room of Eufrasia's house, standing among the dust and chunks of plaster.

"*El dinero,*" he said softly.

That was all he said for a long time. Through the window I could see that the hills in the distance had turned from orange to red.

I went into the bedroom after *Tío* Henry. Alicia sat on the bed, smoothing the pages of the diary. She looked up.

"Margarita is the strongest of us. She always gets her way. You should remember that from our childhood." She handed me the diary and I paged through it.

"How?" he said. "How could she cheat us?"

"I caught her just about to leave. She threatened me with her shoe."

I flipped through the pictures in the diary. A wedding ceremony. Some children posing on the sidewalks of Tijuana. And photos of the fight, with signatures on the backs. The actual knockout. Everything I needed.

Alicia brushed her hair back. "*Niño,* how was the girl's party?"

"All right." I was looking at one of the pictures. *Abuelo* Lupe sending a blow to Dempsey's head.

"I had better go before your *tío* loses control." She lifted her hand to my hair, but then stopped. "I see you've found what you wanted."

I thumbed through the pages to find more pictures. Three of the actual knockout. I could probably give one to Jeremy. And one of Dempsey with his arm around *Abuelo* Lupe. Probably before the fight. And some others that weren't as clear.

When I looked up, Alicia had gone. I tried to read some of the Spanish in the book, but didn't understand most of it. I saw the checks where I had left them. They were all that Margarita had left. I put them in the cover of the book.

I found *Tío* Henry at the *señora's* table again. My mother clenched his arm as he poured another drink. "What is wrong with you? Why must you be so rude?"

When he put the glass to his lips, the rim clicked against his teeth. "We have lost everything," he said. He swirled the drops of liquid at the bottom of the glass.

"No," she said. Her voice was almost cheerful. "You were right. It will be worth it in the end."

"No, *hermanita*."

A few seconds passed. She watched him with a very small smile on her face. Tears came to her eyes. "Everything?" she whispered.

He leaned into his hands. The muscles in his arms never seemed bigger.

I stood between them, put the book on the table. "We can still cash these." I opened it. "About a thousand dollars."

Tío Henry took the checks. He laughed very quietly. "Worthless, *muchacho*. Just like the old woman's scribblings." He closed the book and tossed it to the fire with the checks in it. I jumped up and reached into the flames. I pulled my arm back, waved my empty hand in the air. *Tío* poured another drink and watched the book burn. My mother stared at him, her smile nearly gone. The book went black in the flames, and out of the pages a black smoke rose like a ghost escaping.

We sat without saying anything, watching the fire burn low. The torn piñata twisted back and forth on the clothesline. When the sting had left my hand, I felt my pocket for the fifty-dollar bill. It was there—safe, crisp, and neatly folded.

THE REASON FOR ANGELS

LUCÍA SÁNCHEZ WAS TWENTY MINUTES LATE for her sister Mema's funeral. She had dashed to the cannery for her paycheck, but the bank wouldn't cash it on her overdrawn account. She called the teller a fool and a blockhead in Spanish, then dragged her boys by the shirtsleeves out to the '68 Chevy that *Tío* Luis had lent her from his shop. Clutching her last seven dollars against the steering wheel, she ran all the red and amber lights down Maya Boulevard. Her foot instinctively tapped the brake only for those pedestrians who looked clean-cut and respectable. She gassed right by the *cholos* in red bandanas and the *chicanitas* with too much make-up.

"You're making me ride in a car without seatbelts?" Richie said. He threw himself face-up on the back seat. "You're increasing my chances of death by a factor of two hundred. I don't believe you're my mother."

"Don't be a *mocoso*," Lucía said. She cranked her window up as far as it would go, but hot air still whistled in. Loose hair kicked around her face. "Now think of something to tell your grandparents."

"They're not my grandparents," Richie said. "I'm convinced you adopted me."

"One of these days you'll learn the importance of your family," she said, leaning into the mirror to seek him out. "Only by then, you'll be one of these shiftless *cholitos*. Who's going to have anything to do with you then?"

"Forget it," he said. "This is the last time I wear a tie for those people."

"Why must you always pick the hottest days to aggravate me?"

"You always say 'always,'" Richie said. "It's so imprecise, I can't stand it."

The tires howled as they caught the turn on Seventh. Manuelito kneeled backwards next to her. He held on by a rip in the vinyl. "I wish some mean cops would chase us," he said. "I hope we have an accident."

"Yeah," Richie said. "A real pileup. Put us on the news with that Andy Ramírez that interviews all the spics and wetbacks on TV."

"*Tía* Mema was a TV star," Manuelito said.

Richie curled his knees to his chin in laughter. "A public service announcement for that organization of prudes."

"They help new immigrants get jobs," Lucía said. "What's wrong with that?"

"Nothing, if you like squishing peach wedges into tin cans."

"*Malcriado!*" she said, swatting the bills at what she could see of him in the mirror. "You are not going to embarrass me today."

Richie put his feet up on the armrest and started lighting matches and flicking them out the window. "You know I don't understand you when you speak that language," he said.

"And I won't hesitate to slap you in front of the relatives."

"Yeah," Manuelito said. "Slap you in front of the relatives."

"Shut up," Richie said. "You're so hyper. A real mother wouldn't let you eat so much sugar."

The car skidded into the gravel parking lot of the Goodwill. Manuelito tumbled backwards onto the floor. "Quit horsing around," Lucía said, throwing her door wide.

Inside, she ran down the aisles past the cardboard Women's Apparel sign. The clacking of her shoes echoed in the warehouse-like building. She began to struggle through racks of dresses. Coat hangers clattered. Dresses that weren't black or had low necklines dropped to the floor. Memita, Lucía thought, as soon as I have two spare minutes, I'll cry for you. Now give me some of that fashion advice I never listened to. I don't want to make a fool of myself.

She held up a size eight with a sequined sash and shook it. The wrinkles fell smooth. It was good material, deeply pleated like those designer originals that Mema used to drag her to see at the L.A. fashion shows. "Getups," Lucía would say out loud in Spanish. "Who would wear such things?" Then she would wave her arms dismissively at the pale, stiff models on the runway until her sister almost cried for shame and swore never to speak to her again. But a few days later, Mema would run up her steps with a pair of new tickets pinched between her long red nails.

This dress wasn't so bad, even if it did have those padded, arrogant-looking shoulders that Mema loved to show off in at family gatherings. Lucía used to wait anxiously at Mamá's table to see Mema come swinging through the door without knocking, forty minutes late for dinner, level shoulders thrown back in a snug new business suit. She was the only one who could skip Mamá's special meals, forget a family birthday, or even raise her voice above

Papá's. She got away with these things by silently flashing a new piece of jewelry, which meant another raise, or by sporting a new, very short hairstyle, which meant another promotion. Sometimes, all she had to do was bare her whitest smile—her "success smile," Lucía called it—that seemed to show everyone how far an intelligent, modern-thinking American could rise.

Their cousin Lana once said she had seen Mema in a "lovers' tangle" with one of her bosses at a restaurant in Pasadena, and that that of course explained everything. What was a lovers' tangle? Lucía wanted to know. After much hedging, Lana made Lucía promise not to tell, and said she had seen their ankles touching under the table. Lucía called Mema the next day and they laughed about it for an hour. "It was just one dinner," Mema said. "She's just jealous because we have figures, while she's as flat as Mamá's *tortillas de harina*." From then on, whenever they got together with Lana, Mema would stretch her leg under the table and rub her bare foot against Lucía's leg. The two of them would laugh without restraint until Lana stood up, threw down her napkin, and demanded to know what was so hilarious.

So who's going to be the family businesswoman now? Lucía thought. She held up the dress and tried to see herself in it, but it remained a formless length of material. She had no idea if it would do for a funeral.

I don't have time to argue with you, Memita. She bought the dress and a pair of black shoes for Manuelito and ran out the door.

In the car, she handed Manuelito the shoes and started the engine.

"Why is Mamá crying?" Manuelito said.

"She isn't crying," Richie said. "Is she crying? Well, you have to do that at funerals."

"When we're in the church," Lucía said, wiping her eyes, "I don't want any fighting between you two."

"I'll wait in the car," Richie said. "Maybe my real family will pass by and claim me."

"You're not going to humiliate me," Lucía said.

"Why do we have to go in there and pretend like she was some kind of angel?"

"Your grandparents are waiting."

"There was so much gossip," Richie said. "Everyone knew about it."

"Your cousins from Mexico City are going to be there." She pulled into the church lot and drove to the back where the catechism school was. She began struggling into the dress in the front seat. "If you don't go, that's the end of your allowance."

"Gasp. Choke," Richie said. "Threat of further destitution."

She reached over the seat to slap him.

"Take your best shot. Win a prize."

"Do it for me," she said.

"Forget it."

"Please."

"She gave me Golden Books until I was eleven."

Lucía got out and slammed the door. A watery feeling went through her legs and she leaned against the car for a minute, until the shaking had stopped.

On the far side of the cemetery stood the tall eucalyptus trees. She couldn't feel a breeze, but the warm scent of the trees came to her, as if carried on the strains of church organ music. It was like the most expensive of Mema's perfumes, the one she had lent Lucía once, saying, "This will change who you are, if you let it. You don't believe me? You have to start from the outside and work in, Lucia."

Lucía closed her eyes and breathed in the strong, sweet smell.

"You're not crying again, are you?" Richie said. He stuck his head out the window. "Please, Mom. Don't cry."

"Look at that," she said after a minute. She had turned to her reflection in the window of one of the catechism classrooms. She ran her hands over the soft material at her waist. "I'm a size ten, but this doesn't look too bad. It's not tight." She put her hands on her hips and twisted to get a side view.

"Let me see," Richie said. "It looks fine. You need to fix your hair, it's all over your face." He leaned out the window and brushed the damp hair away from her mouth, then straightened the sash of her dress.

Tío Luis came running down the back steps of the church, waving a white handkerchief as if to signal that everything was safe inside.

"Don't make me one of them," Richie said, leaning almost all the way out. "Don't you see how it is?"

Tío Luis was breathing hard as he came up, the way Lucía had sometimes seen him do when he was hard at work repairing cars.

"They're not going to wait much longer," he said, taking Lucía's arm. "Oh, *pobrecita,* take my hanky. That's better. But you're not going to believe it. I still don't believe it. I'm doing the best I can in there. but I don't know how long I can keep it up."

"What are you talking about?" Lucía said.

"*He's* here. *He* showed up." He took another handkerchief from his breast pocket and patted his big moustache.

"Who?" Lucía said.

"*Him,*" he whispered.

"*No me digas,*" she said, covering her mouth with the cloth.

"I told you you wouldn't believe it," he said, lifting Manuelito through the window. He swung him under his arm like an empty tool box. Lucía started to run after him.

"I want to listen to the radio," Richie said. "Leave me the keys."

"In the ignition," she called back.

Mema, I told you and told you and told you. I don't *want* to meet this man of your dreams.

🙦 🙦 🙦

She waited behind the wreaths in the vestibule, picking at the chrysanthemums and bruising them between her fingers. When the organ gave a peal that was loud enough and long enough, she rushed to the last pew unnoticed.

She looked over the neatly combed heads of hair and the women's black hats. Everyone looked too much the same from behind. None of them looked like the man who had been Mema's boss at the company. Four cousins from Mexico City filled one of the front pews with Mamá and Papá, as if traveling all that distance entitled them to the best seats. They had often complained in letters to Mamá about how expensive it was to visit the U.S., but Lucía couldn't remember them ever having missed a funeral. When *Tío* Pedro died, she had overheard them chattering with some of their younger American cousins out on Pedro's lawn about his gambling. The old man had been arrested in a police raid on one of the local cockfights, and this was great news to them. Now they sat holding their heads up like expectant movie-goers waiting for the lights to dim.

Tío Luis was wandering up and down the aisles with Manuelito, passing out handkerchiefs like a nurse handing out bandages to the injured. He moved deftly up and down the pews in spite of his size, giving hugs and words of condolence. He picked Manuelito up in his hefty arms to show him off to some of the aunts, tipping him over the side of the pew as if he were pouring water from a jar. He was giving them something else to talk about, a distraction.

She still hadn't seen the man. But what was his name? Now that she thought of it, she didn't even know what he looked like. She had refused to listen to Mema talk about him while helping her move into the new Oceanside apartment that he and Mema had rented. Mema had hit the emergency stop on the way up and the elevator had jolted to a standstill.

"I can't believe the gossip bothers you," she had said. "In school, they said 'She gets A's by kissing up.' When I went to Mexico by myself, they said 'She flattered *Tío* Luis for the money.' Now they say 'She sleeps her way to the top.' When did you start believing that kind of nonsense?"

"I never believed any of those things," Lucía had said.

"What, then?"

"He's *married*," she'd said, clutching a heavy box to her breast.

"Look at me," Mema had said. "Can't you see he means everything to me?"

"I don't want to hear anymore," Lucía had said, trying to turn away. "And *please* don't tell me he has kids."

Tío Luis brought Manuelito back.

"Where is he?" she said.

"*Querida, estamos en una situación muy precaria.*" My dear, we're in a tight spot.

"Why?" Lucía said. "What's the matter?"

"*Delante de Usted.*"

She looked at the person in front of her. "Are you sure? How do you know?"

"Who else could it be?" he whispered, still in Spanish. "If that's not him, then that's one pale Mexican who's come to the wrong mass."

Manuelito started kicking his legs back and forth.

"Do you have to pee?" she said.

"Where is *Tía*?" he said. "Is she late for this too?"

"I told you," she said. "She's gone to Heaven. She's an angel there now."

"Why do they have angels there?"

"I don't know why. They just do." She took a chocolate square from her purse and gave it to him. She leaned towards *Tío* Luis. "Well? Are you going to do something?"

"No," he said. "Everything is running smoothly. I know when to stop tinkering." He took out a plastic package. "Do you need another hanky? I brought plenty."

Lucía scooted down the pew to get a better view of the man. She could see straight over his head, which was graying behind the ears. She was sure he would have been much more handsome—dangerously handsome, and tall, like the cheats and liars in the black-and-white matinee shows. But this man could have been Lucía's pharmacist, or mailman. His face was pink and smoothly shaven, with long, thin cheekbones and a mole at the corner of his mouth, as if he had dotted himself by accident with a black ink pen. Lucía leaned forward and saw that he was twisting his watch band with a hooked pinky, the way Mema did with her bracelets when she was nervous. People were always picking up her bad habits. But also like Mema, even in a crowd of unfamiliar people he held his head up and his shoulders back. A tear went down his face.

"I can't sit here," Lucía said. She stepped over Manuelito and *Tío* Luis and went up to the front of the church. She stopped Mamá and Papá as they came out of their pew. Mamá leaned against her, crying. Lucía and Papá helped her to the front railing.

"It's okay, Mamá. She's gone to God."

They kneeled together. Papá said nothing and didn't look at Lucia. He took a place at the railing on the other side of Mamá.

"He's not going to speak to me until Easter, is he?" Lucía said when Mamá had steadied herself at the rail and was quiet.

"You were late," she said. "What did you expect?"

"Tell him I'm sorry," Lucía said.

Mamá gripped the rail. The blue veins in her hands darkened. "Who is that little *gringo* at the back?"

"Nobody," Lucía said.

"Good," she said. She patted Lucía's hand once, lightly. "That's what I thought."

Lucía folded her hands and started to pray, but didn't know what to pray for. She touched the casket in front of her, the gold paint gliding under her fingertips. Freshly cut lilies had been placed on the platform around the casket. The cut ends dripped blots onto the red cloth. The white mouths of the flowers opened towards her, as if they had something to tell her. She stood and leaned over her sister.

The dress was unlike anything she had ever seen Mema wear. The collar was stiff white lace that gathered at her chin. The hem reached her ankles. The cut of the dress made her hips look squarish and uncomfortable. Lucía ran her hands over her own hips. She touched Mema's cheek apologetically, then brushed Mema's short hair behind her ears the way she used to keep it. Mema's hands were folded over her breast, as if ashamed of her appearance. Lucía didn't blame her. Even I have better taste than that, she thought. The dress reminded her of one that Mema had torn to shreds when she was twelve because it was a church dress, not like what the girls at school were wearing. When they were older, Mema would always point out clothes she didn't like in store windows, toss her head back in pretend disgust, and say, "What an ugly sack! You wouldn't catch me dead in it."

Lucía started to laugh quietly. Mamá looked up at her. She laughed until she almost wheezed for air, then had to laugh out loud.

"What is it?" Mamá said. "What are you smiling about?"

"You wouldn't understand," Lucía said. She went back down the center aisle.

Tío Luis had moved to another pew with Manuelito. "Take a looky at Lana," he said. "Tell me what you notice."

Lucía saw her cousin in the crowd, one hand on her hip, the other gesticulating high over her head. Her broad round hat, like a giant record, bobbed up and down as she spoke. Lucía could hear her all the way across the church. "Same old Lana," she said.

"Wait until she holds still," *Tío* Luis said. "There. Did you see it?"

"See what?"

"*La nariz,*" he said. "I think she's had another nose job."

"Don't be ridiculous," she said. "She looks the same."

"Ah ha!" he whispered, slapping his knee. "That's because she's having it done in stages. She doesn't want the family to notice. And look at those pointies." He held up a wad of handkerchiefs. "She's been padding those titties for years."

Lana saw Lucía looking at her. She threw her a kiss that could have gone all the way to Canada, then went back to talking.

After the mass Lana trotted over in her spiked heels, arms outstretched. She took a tiny bit of pink gum from her mouth and pressed it daintily behind her ear lobe, then hugged Lucia. "What a sad time!" Lana said, almost shrieking. She wouldn't let Lucía go.

"We all loved her," Lucía said. She could smell the cinnamon on Lana's ear.

"I couldn't stand her," Lana said. "But you loved her and that's what really matters. I was always too jealous."

"But look at you," Lucía said, finally breaking away and holding her at arm's length. "Everyone should be jealous of you. You're a big success, a big time stewardess."

"A flight attendant," Lana said, sitting down. "And my feet are killing me." She unstrapped her shoes and kicked them off. She took Lucía's hand and leaned towards her. "I feel so bad. How you must be suffering with *him* here. Don't play dumb, Lucía. I saw you and *Tío*—hello, *Tío,* how are you—

I saw you talking right behind his back. Do you want me to kick him out of here? I'll go right over . . ."

"No," Lucía said. "It's fine."

"What do you mean fine? Who does he think he is?"

"He's not causing any trouble, Lana."

"What are you, a saint? Go over there and slap his face."

"I think he's going to leave soon."

"Then go ask him for a job. Get something from him, he owes it to you. He owes it to Mema. Threaten to tell his wife on him."

"I'm not going to make a scene," Lucía said.

"Think of how proud your parents would be. You could get out of that cannery once and for all."

"I don't have any experience," Lucía said.

"You have experience supervising."

"I had an offer to supervise, but they wouldn't let me have overtime. I needed the money from overtime."

"He has to give you a job," Lana said. She looked over her shoulder. "Look at him. What a weasel. I'll go ask him for you, nice and casual."

"No! I'm going outside. I need air."

"I wouldn't go out there," Lana said. "There's some kid burning rubber in the parking lot. I almost got killed."

🐚 🐚 🐚

"How was it?" Richie said. He was lying on the hood of the Chevy with his shirt off and his tie over his eyes. "Am I any darker yet?"

"What kind of trouble have you been in?" Lucía said. Dozens of long black arcs and overlapping circles covered the parking lot. "You're not old enough to drive."

"I have to learn sometime," he said.

A girl in black velvet was walking towards them from the first group of people that had come out of the church. Lucía hoped Mema's boss had gone out the back way.

"¿Es Usted la Señora Sánchez?" the girl said.

"That's my mom all right," Richie said. "But if you're looking for a ride, I wouldn't risk it."

"¿Es Usted la Señora Sánchez?"

"Cute," Richie said. "Too bad no English."

The girl said her name was Sarita. She said that her aunt, Lucía's cousin from Mexico, was too sick to come to the funeral, but sent her condolences and her love. Lucía nodded.

At the top of the church steps Lana was talking to someone. She dangled her high heels from her fingertips. When she turned sideways, her big hat uncovered the man with the graying hair.

Lucía held her purse tight against her stomach. She told Sarita that she was glad to have met her, and that she would see her later at the gathering. Lana was leading the man by the hand down the steps.

"Get in the car," she said to Richie. She opened the door for Manuelito and helped him in.

Lana let go of his hand and started running in her stockings. He followed her. "Lucía," she said in her sweetest, highest voice. "This is Mr. Russell."

They looked at each other and said nothing. Relatives passed through the parking lot in small black clusters. Several heads were turned over their shoulders, eyes shielded against the sun. Lucía could feel it hot on her back.

"I'll leave you to talk," Lana said. She squeezed Lucía's hand. "I'll see you at your mother's. I have something to show you."

Lucía and the man stood alone together. She wanted her first words to be the coldest ones she had ever spoken. She wanted him to leave. She could see how hard he tried to hold the tears back, the edges of his eyelids turning bright red and wet.

"You loved her," she said.

He lifted his hands upwards slightly, as if to hug her and to say, "I couldn't help it" at the same time. His tie was crooked and Lucía couldn't help wanting to fix it.

"I heard what you said to your boy," he said. "About Mema being an angel. That's the way I think of her. Will you talk to me for a few minutes?"

"No," Lucía said. Faces she hardly recognized were watching from car windows. "Maybe. Call me at home." She hurried to the other side of the Chevy and got in. She started the engine.

"I want you to understand something clearly," she said to Richie as she drove towards the street. Her Spanish was rarely so well pronounced. "You're going to the gathering after the burial . . ."

"Not this again," Richie said.

"Shut up," she said. "You're going, and you'll sit there and be quiet and not embarrass me. Got it?"

"I guess so," he said, looking out the rear windshield as they pulled out of the lot.

"Your grandfather is going to see that I know how to raise a couple of decent children. And when I introduce you to people, stand up straight and don't roll your eyes when I tell them how good you're doing in school. And it wouldn't hurt if you said a few things in Spanish, especially to your grandfather."

"That's where I draw the line," Richie said. "I don't speak that language."

When they were on the freeway again, he sat up on the back seat and put his tie back on. "How do you say, 'You're really good-looking' in Spanish?" he said. "I mean, without getting slapped in the face?"

✿✿ ✿✿ ✿✿

Lana was standing in the middle of the living room, telling the cousins from Mexico City about how she had been sure she was going to die in a take-off collision just last week. They leaned forward on Mamá's sofa as Lana waved her hands in the air and clapped them together to indicate an explosion.

Lucía handed her a plate of *chiles rellenos* and they sat down together. "How awful," she said. "How do you bear it?"

"Oh," Lana said, crossing her legs. She flung her hat on the coffee table. "That's nothing. Everytime I go up, I'm positive it's the end of everything. But as long as I keep smiling, nobody notices."

Richie was already trying to talk to Sarita in the kitchen. At least he wasn't in a corner by himself giving everyone mean looks. *Tío* Luis bounced Manuelito on his knee to keep him quiet.

"So?" Lana said. "Is he going to arrange something for you?"

"I only had a minute to talk to him" Lucía said.

"How much longer did you want? Tell me what he said."

"He didn't offer anything."

"And you didn't ask." She snatched Lucía's plate away from her, grabbed her hand and jerked her out of the sofa. She pulled her down to the end of the hallway.

"I've been wanting to show you something," she said. She pulled her dress down over her shoulders as if she were tearing Christmas wrapping from a package. She loosened her bra and took Lucía's hand. "Feel," she said. "Squeeze."

"What is it?" Lucía said, touching the breasts lightly.

"These are real," she said. "These are me. It took me a year to pay for them, but they helped get me my first job."

"Oh my God," Lucía said, pulling away.

"It was God that had me working in the shoe factory while your sister never had to chip a nail. It's me that got me where I am now." She took Lucía's hand. "If I didn't care two hairs for your stupid sister, I cared twice as much about you. I don't want to see you stuck where I was."

Lucía laid both palms gently on Lana's breasts.

"They're kind of pretty, no?"

In the living room they cleared away the dishes and sat down next to each other. Lana took out a stick of gum and Manuelito came up and asked for some. Lana showed him her empty hands. "All gone," she said, even though she always carried three or four extra packs in her purse to keep her breath fresh.

Lucía took out a piece of chocolate for him.

"Oh," Lana said. "That's so bad for his teeth. You shouldn't let him."

"I like it," Manuelito said.

"Wait until you're fat and have a lot of pimples," she said. "The girls will all run away from you screaming their heads off. Then you'll want to kill yourself."

Lucía went into the kitchen to help with the *chiles rellenos*. "Mamá," she said. "Let somebody else do this."

"It keeps me calm," she said, dipping the *chiles* into the batter. "I want you to do something for me. Go see who that is in the car across the street."

Through the curtains Lucía saw a man in a red Datsun checking his watch. The sun drummed on her forehead through the window. She snapped the curtains shut. "It's nobody."

"I know it's nobody. See what Nobody wants and ask him to leave." The batter hissed in the grease.

"Did you see Richie?" Lucía said. "He's actually speaking Spanish with Sarita. I can't believe it."

Mamá turned the flame up on the stove. The hissing got louder.

Lucía closed the back door carefully behind her, then went around the house and far enough into the driveway that she couldn't see the living room windows. She pulled her hair back and crossed her arms. Four or five cars passed in each direction before he saw her.

"You have to get out of here," she called.

He draped his long, pale fingers over the car door. "I just wanted to talk to you," he said. "For a minute."

"I told you. You can call."

He turned his palms towards the sky and shrugged.

"The phone book," Lucía said.

One hand slipped out of sight and she heard the lock of his door pop. She stepped onto the sidewalk. "Please, not now."

"Lana said you needed a job. That's why I came."

"I have a job," she said, stepping into the hot street. "I don't need anything."

"Please," he said. "Anything I can do."

A van made the turn around the corner as Lucía moved forward. It passed close behind her, the air ruffling her dress. He started to open his door.

"All right," she said. "Just don't get out."

"I appreciated what you said at the church," he said once she was in. He laid his fingers gently over the steering wheel and gazed through it. "You look like her. In that dress."

"I'm very sorry," she said, touching his wrist. "I don't know what else I can say to you. My family is waiting for me."

"I don't . . ."

She looked past him and out his window. The curtains in the house were all drawn shut. "You don't what?"

"Have anybody. To talk to."

Lucía breathed deeply and folded her hands. "Maybe God took Mema so you could be with your wife. My mother says there's always a reason for these things. Sometimes there is."

He gripped the wheel as if struggling not to cry. "Left," he said. "Months ago."

There was a movement in the living room curtains. Lucía turned away, but he locked her door from his side. He kept his finger on the button.

"Let me out," she said.

"What Mema said about you is true. She would have wanted me to help you."

"Then call me." She tried the door again. "Call me."

"You're not listed."

She opened the glove compartment and found a pen. She wrote her number on the back of an envelope. She shoved it to the back of the dashboard.

"How am I going to live without her?" He started to cry, but kept his finger hard against the lock button. Faces appeared in the living room window.

She tried the door again. He reached out to grab her arm. She slapped his hand away. Hair fell across her face. She pulled at the door handle and got out, catching her heel in the weeds on the curb. She left the door open and ran into the street. His door slammed and he was right behind her.

"Wait," he said. "I didn't mean anything."

She turned around in the middle of the street and caught her breath. "I know you didn't," she said. She stepped towards him. They were quiet for a minute. "Call me about the job," she said. "I want it."

She waited for him to drive off, then went back inside.

She closed the screen door behind her. Only Richie and Sarita's voices could be heard in the kitchen. She could see the door to Papá's room had been shut. For the first time, Lucía noticed her family's clothes. It was as if everyone had just changed into black. *Tío* Luis stood up and put his arms around her, and she leaned into him, letting him rock her gently back and forth.

Lucía went into the kitchen where Mamá was still fixing the peppers that no one was going to eat. At the refrigerator, Lucía poured herself a glass of ice water, feeling the cold instantly through the glass. She stood in the doorframe with her feet wide apart and one hand on her hip. She wiped her forearm across her brow and took a long, slow drink from the glass.

HARD LANGUAGE

THEY HAD BEEN LIVING LEGALLY in the United States for a year and a half when Antonio announced to his wife in no uncertain terms that they were going to learn English once and for all.

"We know less now than we did when we moved here," he said, pacing the border of the frayed oval rope rug. "There's no way we're going to get ahead if we don't know the language."

On the sofa Pilar thumbed through one of her Mexican movie magazines while *menudo* simmered in the kitchen. "And where am I going to find time to take a class?" she said. "I have this house to take care of and you to cook for and the neighbor's kids to watch in the afternoons."

"Most of my customers are going to speak English," he went on. "There's no way I can grow the business otherwise."

"Fine." She snapped her magazine shut. "Get me my own car so I don't have to walk half an hour to get groceries, and plan on cooking some of your own meals, and get the building manager to finally fix that washing machine. Then I'll take your class."

She went into the kitchen and gave the *menudo* a forceful stir, took it off the stove and turned down the flame. At the table she laid out a bowl and spoon for each of them and a plate of olives from the Greek store downstairs. They sat down. Steam rose up between them, a gauzy curtain.

"There's one more thing," Antonio said, tucking his napkin into his shirt. "If we're going to do this, we have to do it right. No more Mexican movies and Mexican radio and Mexican newspapers. Everything is going to have to be in English from now on."

She ladled out the soup, shaking her head as if listening to a lunatic's ramblings.

"Pilar, look at the Pachecos. They've been here for five years and they still can't say anything. Why? Because they only talk Spanish around the house, they only have Mexican friends."

"So now you want me to give up my friends, too? Maybe I could also bleach my hair and eyebrows. That way I'd look *and* sound like an American."

Antonio cleared his throat. "In the long run, Pilar—"

"How is it you know what's best 'in the long run'?"

"I want us to make progress."

"Leaving Tijuana was supposed to be progress."

"We had nothing in Tijuana."

"We had our own house."

"It was your parent's house."

"At least it wasn't a moldy shoe-box, and at least we had more to eat than watered-down . . ."

"Pilar!" He pounded his fist on the table so his soup splattered. He did not wipe it up.

She pursed her lips. Dark lines radiated out from the corners of her mouth, her eyes. Then she threw her twisted napkin on the table and left the room.

When she came back a few minutes later, she had her hair pulled back into a ponytail. "All right," she said. "I'll sign us up for the class tomorrow. But don't expect more than baloney sandwiches for dinner and don't come griping to me when you find you don't have enough clean shirts for the week."

Antonio's heart swelled with gratitude, but he kept his head lowered, his face somber. From the day they got married, he had asked more of her than it had been fair to expect. Trying to start his own scrap business while working at O'Connor's machine shop meant they hadn't spent a weekend together in six months, and it had been more than a year since they had returned to Tijuana to visit her parents. That night in bed, Antonio slipped his leg between hers. He wanted to make love to her, to show her how much he appreciated her. But she only moved to her edge of the bed with her arms wrapped tightly around a pillow.

In the morning, they rose and showered together without talking. She scrambled his eggs and *chorizo* in the kitchen, working the pan with violent motions, her lips clamped in a bitter smile. He chose to leave her alone. Women were entitled to periods of extreme anger and sadness, and he had learned it was best to indulge them. The inner workings of their hearts were intricate and fine—too delicate to be tampered with by clumsy men.

On Friday of that week, he came home from work to find Pilar chirping happily on the phone with her mother. She waved to Antonio, then got off the phone quickly to greet him with a kiss. He put his arms around her, buried his face in her hair. "Did something good happen to you today?" he said.

"Nothing in particular. Maybe it's just because today is the first day of spring. You know how nice weather affects me."

But Antonio noticed something different about her that night as she started dinner. For a long time he couldn't pinpoint what it was. Not until he asked her if she needed help and she waved him away from the counter did he figure it out. Pilar was smiling in the kitchen. He had never noticed it before, but now he realized Pilar never smiled in the kitchen. She hated to cook, and normally grumbled and clattered and thrashed her way through preparing even the simplest meals. But today she was smiling, like someone on the cover of a homemaking magazine.

She smiled throughout dinner, too, then hummed through the clearing of plates. From the sofa in the living room he watched her carefully, the way she nearly danced to secret music in her head from counter to cupboard. It wasn't until later, when she stepped out to see her friend Monica but did not come back for nearly two hours, that Antonio's thoughts, like iron shavings to a magnet, adhered themselves to the possibility that Pilar was having an affair.

It had happened once before, while they were still living in Tijuana in a brown-faced cottage Pilar's parents had rented for them on the east side of town. Over the side-yard fence Antonio had seen Pilar walking towards the house with a delicate-jawed, sleek-haired young man who owned the grocery store down the street. Their shoulders brushed as they ambled along. What had ensued from Antonio's accusation was a single, unending night of tables pounded and doors slammed, faces contorted in rage and words honed to murderous pitch. Yes, she finally admitted, she had spent the day with him at the movies. But she had come from an active family of seven children, was not accustomed to spending her days alone, and anyway, if Antonio had taken her to the movies the weekend before as he had promised to in the first place . . . No, she said, there was nothing between them, he was just a boy, for God's sake. After hours of argument had exhausted them to the point of gray numbness, they at last sat across from each other in the haggard dawn, and came to an agreement: They would accelerate their plans to move to the United States. And in return, he would never again accuse her of something of which he had no proof.

✿ ✿ ✿

"Why so serious today, Antonio?" Miguel said. He was standing on a crate at his lathe in the machine shop, being too short to reach it himself. "Problems with the wife, maybe?"

Antonio smiled, but concentrated on his lathe, fitting the shaft into the chuck.

"You should have seen the one I had last night," Miguel said, loud enough for everyone in the warehouse to hear.

"How does anyone so short and pudgy get so many women?" Gómez, one of the other workers, shouted.

"And with dragon breath on top of it," someone else said.

"I have what women want," Miguel said. He held a nine-inch length of shaft up over his head and shook it. There was a burst of laughter. Someone threw a turning at him, but he deflected it with his arm. "And you know what the best thing about her was? She was married. Married women in unhappy relationships are always the wildest."

"What about the poor husbands?" someone said.

"They should thank me," he said. "After all, I'm doing them a service, returning their wives to them satisfied and in a good mood . . . ."

Antonio slammed the off button on his machine and tore off his goggles. The compressor whirred to a stop. He headed towards the rest room. Miguel followed him.

"What is it, *hombre?*" he said. "Something's gotten into you today."

"You shouldn't talk that way," Antonio said.

"I wasn't serious," he said. "I just make these things up. You know, to make the time go faster."

"But you have cheated with married women, haven't you?"

"Well, sure. And Carmela used to cheat on me too. Everybody does it."

Antonio said nothing, only stared at his shoes.

"Listen," Miguel said. "You're my best friend. I don't want to offend you. If it will make you feel better, I'll try to tone things down a little."

Antonio thought for a moment. "Tell me, is there a way to tell if a woman is cheating on you?"

"Ah," Miguel said. "It's in the touch. Like when your chuck isn't tightened right. You can't tell by looking, but you can feel it in your hands."

❧ ❧ ❧

That night Antonio came up behind Pilar in the bathroom and as carefully as if he were conducting the most delicate of experiments, put his arms around her. The curves of her body yielded into his, like molten metal filling its cast. Surely she couldn't have responded this way if she had recently been with another.

But moments later she was on her way out to the dry cleaners to pick up something that she said she'd forgotten there earlier.

"Do you know where the *TV Guide* is?" he said to get her attention.

She stopped in the door frame, with one foot in the living room, one foot out in the hall. "It probably fell between the cushions," she said, but she did not come back in to help him find it. Instead, she glanced over her shoulder— not at him, but at the clock above his head.

Antonio felt his heart cool to a solid. He could not move, as his suspicions swirled up around him. He imagined a man waiting for her—in a parked car, a hotel room, an office. He pictured him looking at his watch, wondering what was keeping her. Pictured Pilar's nervous, bird-like stride as she hurried to be on time.

Antonio sat for a long time after Pilar was gone, watching his own distorted reflection in the curved TV tube which was not on—the face of an imbecile, a fool. Then he left the house and started to walk. He walked west of the commercial district and under the freeway, then out past the train tracks to where a stale wind was sweeping over barren fields. He walked quickly to keep the images from overtaking him, spiky cattails catching in his pant cuffs. Something painful and watery rose in his throat. He wanted to be where no one would see him should he start to cry. But no sooner was he alone than he felt a desperate need to be among the living. He turned back. Perhaps if he wandered long enough he would find her, catch her coming out of an unknown apartment, see *him* waving goodbye from an unfamiliar doorstep. Is that what he was hoping for? What would he do then? To her? To him?

His mind was beginning to grow numb when he passed the Bal Theatre, where Spanish-language movies played along with American films dubbed into Spanish. He had passed it once already. But now fear spilled out of him, leaving him a clear, quivering, embarrassed shell. He knew exactly where she was.

He bought a ticket without looking to see what was playing and went into the theatre. The girl in the tubular box office window called out that the next showing was not for another hour, but Antonio kept walking. There was no one in the lobby to take his ticket, so he walked into the theatre.

He found Pilar in the back row where she usually liked to sit, her coat drawn over her lap against the theatre chill. He sat down next to her, but she did not notice him. The border of the screen trembled unevenly, but at its center a smartly-dressed man and woman held each other firmly. Was that Claudia Beltrán, the star of their teen years that they had gone to see when they'd first been dating? He couldn't remember, but he thought so. Antonio felt his own heart blossom against the inside of his rib cage. Or was it only the orchestra's swelling violins that were making him feel this way?

He touched Pilar's hand and she jumped. "¡Ay! Antonio! Why are you here?" In a rushed whisper she began to explain, but he stopped her by pressing his lips to the back of her hand. His penitent tears dripped onto her wrist. He threaded his fingers through hers, marveling at the fit, a fist in his throat blocking words.

He did not let her talk as they walked home. It was dark by now. In the clear and glittering sky he saw reflected the state of his own heart. "I'll take you to the Spanish movies any time you want," he said. "I don't know what I was thinking. I never meant to be so harsh, Pilar."

That night sweet guilt fueled his lovemaking with her. He did for her all the things she liked, poured favorite words into her ears, the ones that made her arch her back and strain her toes as if trying to touch something just the other side of this world. Maybe it was a mistake to concede so completely, but . . . there was no "but." There was only this, only Pilar, only now.

❧ ❧ ❧

The English class took place in the gymnasium at the local high school. The teacher, a boy-faced man of about twenty-five with James Dean sideburns, arrived to class in a knitted sweater with the print of a parrot spreading its wings against a sunrise. Immediately Antonio did not like him. He was too young and obviously spent too much time caring for his appearance. He moved about the room too energetically and taught with elaborate gestures that Antonio thought were unnecessary and effeminate. Antonio sat silently through the first class, gnawing his pen cap into a gnarled lump.

"I think the teacher's a fag," he told Pilar afterwards. She was sitting on the living room floor starting their first assignment, legs tucked under the glass coffee table.

"He's a good teacher," she said. She adjusted her black-framed reading glasses, but didn't look up.

"How can you say that? It's only the first class. He hasn't had a chance to teach us anything."

"I can tell, that's all."

"You like him because he's attractive," he said.

"I like him because he's interesting." She took Antonio's hand and pulled him down to the floor with her. "Come sit. We can do the first assignment together."

He scooted close to her, flipped through the first few pages. "Admit you think he's attractive," he said after a few minutes.

"I think *you're* attractive," she said. She took off her glasses and circled her fingers around the back of his neck, but he resisted her kiss. He hated it whenever Pilar condescended to him. With his broad flat nose and pocked moon face, he often wondered what Pilar had ever seen in him. Since his childhood, his father had constantly reminded him that he was both dense and ugly. "Plan on making your living with your hands rather than your brains," he used to advise. "And don't be picky when it comes to choosing a wife. A face like yours is more likely to attract flies than women."

The next week the teacher went up and down the rows asking each student to read a few sentences aloud, stopping each person every few minutes to correct pronunciation. But when he got to Pilar, he did not stop her. He let her read for several minutes. Then he broke out into slow, deliberate applause. "Thank you, Pilar. You pronounce beautifully."

Pilar sucked in her lower lip and blushed behind her curtain of black hair. Antonio thought he had never seen her look so beautiful. Others were looking at her as well, and some of the guys continued to gaze at her long after the teacher's attention had turned elsewhere. During the break, Antonio moved his desk flush against hers and held her hand throughout the rest of the class.

But as the hour came to an end, Antonio could tell the class was going to be more difficult for him. Trying to speak English had always been like trying to tie a cherry stem into a knot with his tongue. His mistakes seemed to echo louder and reverberate longer in the huge building than anyone else's. He left class with a burning face, his insides knotted with humiliation.

"Don't you see he's after you?" he said to Pilar later. "The way he looks at you, they way he leans against your desk."

"I thought you said he was a fag," Pilar said.

"Even a fag has to notice someone like you," he said.

She started piling up her books.

"Where are you going?" he said.

"Someplace where I can concentrate. You're being ridiculous, and I'm not listening to you anymore."

He followed her to the bedroom. "He likes you," he said.

"Because I'm a good student," she said.

"What's that supposed to mean?"

"Whatever you want."

"You think I'm stupid."

"I think it wouldn't hurt if you studied a little instead of making up fantasies."

At the bathroom door she laid a hand on his chest and pushed him back, then shut the door and locked it. "I'm not stupid," he said, rattling the doorknob. "And I'm telling you, he is after you."

At the shop, Miguel pulled him aside just as Antonio was breaking for lunch. "There are going to be layoffs soon," he said.

"Everybody knows about that," Antonio said. "Why are you whispering?"

Miguel looked over his shoulder. He waddled over to the far side of the silver food truck, gesturing for Antonio to follow him. "I know you're starting your own business. I want to be a part of it."

Antonio shrugged. "I only have two accounts so far. Anyway, you have nothing to worry about. You've been here longer than anyone else."

"And you think I want to be popping out bolts and nuts for the rest of my life?" He pulled Antonio closer by his sleeve. "When the layoffs come, I want to be first in line. You're going to need someone to drive for you and weld boxes and load scrap. And I may be short, but I'm strong as a horse and I have stamina."

"I wouldn't be able to pay you anything until I got a few more accounts."

"In the long run it will be worth it."

"What about your alimony payments?"

"I can barely pay them now."

Antonio thought for a moment. "Are you willing to take that kind of chance?"

"I've always said you're the only Mexican around here with any vision," he said. "I have a lot of faith in you."

❦ ❦ ❦

On the last day of class, Antonio hurried through the final test. He did not care how he did on it, just as long as he could get out of that classroom once and for all. He turned in his test without looking at the teacher, then rushed out to the parking lot to smoke a cigarette while he waited for Pilar.

A night breeze rushed over them as they walked to dinner that evening to celebrate. "Thank you for taking the class," he said.

He took her hand and tried to go on. There was much more to tell her, but the words struggled against each other, canceling each other in his throat. At the Italian restaurant near their apartment, the waiter seated them outside at one of the patio tables. Insects buzzed about their heads. Antonio tried again. "You made quite an impression on the class."

Pilar bit thoughtfully into a piece of garlic bread. "I was surprised myself. I wasn't expecting it to be that easy."

"Then you're glad I suggested it?"

"I can admit when I'm wrong."

"Yes," he said, "I appreciate that."

He opened his menu, but Pilar didn't open hers. Instead, she took a course catalogue out of her straw bag. "Should we do Wednesday nights again next semester?" she said.

"I thought we would wait a while before we took another class," he said.

"Why shouldn't we keep going?"

"I don't have time now. The layoffs are coming, and I want to have the business built up."

"I thought you needed it for the business."

"I know enough to get by," he said, fumbling his napkin.

"You'll forget everything if you don't practice."

"We can practice at home. We can practice right now."

Pilar looked up.

"We'll take the class in the summer," he said.

"Never mind. I'll just take it myself."

"I'd rather you didn't take it without me."

"Fine." She took up her menu, glared relentlessly into the fold. Over the top of it, the line in her brow darkened.

Antonio picked at the knobby corners of his napkin. Pilar looked around the restaurant, but not at him. She waved the waiter over.

She was silent on the way home. She went into the building while he walked to the corner for a pack of cigarettes. It was always best to give her time to cool off. But when he came in, she was pacing intensely.

"Pilar, please don't be this way."

She turned to him with arms locked in a fold. "I've put up with a lot since we got married," she said. "I've agreed to give up a lot of my time and rearranged my life to learn this stupid language, and now that you see how much I like it, you want to take it away from me. How much more do I have to give up, Antonio? And when do I get to see something in return?"

"It's just that we're married and I think we should do things together."

As she paced, the very air she walked through seemed to boil up around her.

"Pilar, calm down, you're behaving like a child . . ."

Then she did something that she had never before done in their three years of marriage. She picked up a casserole dish and threw it. It glanced off the counter between the kitchen and the dining area and crashed into the glass coffee table. Glass shards spewed everywhere, dispersing the light into a brief, angry rainbow.

✺ ✺ ✺

"When a woman starts to act up it means she's getting her own ideas," Miguel told him after work the next day. Antonio hadn't wanted to go home and had convinced Miguel to have a beer with him. "Have you thought about hitting her? I don't believe in hitting women, of course. But wives . . . well, that's something different."

"Did you ever hit your ex-wife?"

"Of course," he said. "Why do you think she's my ex-wife?"

"So what kind of advice is that?"

"You didn't say you wanted advice."

"Now I'm telling you."

"What about cheating on her?"

"What good would that do?"

"It would get your mind off her."

Antonio rotated his glass between his palms. Miguel gave a long sigh. "There's only one option left, then. You're going to have to swallow your pride and make it up to her."

"I can't seem weak," Antonio said.

"You have a point."

"Then what should I do?"

"Buy me another beer."

"I already bought you two."

"I think better after three."

They kept drinking until the bar closed. Antonio found Pilar at home curled on her side of the bed, fast asleep. It felt good to slip into the warm sheets with her. He guided the hair away from her face so he could look at her, hoping not to wake her, and at the same time hoping she would wake, that she would turn to him and embrace him as if nothing had ever been bad between them. She stirred. Antonio mouthed a wordless prayer that she not tear away from him.

She stirred again, murmured—his name, or something else? "Don't be mad at me," he whispered. She backed into the curve of him, and he slipped his arm around her. Into her ear he whispered one of the phrases that he knew excited her. This was one of the things they both loved—the exchange of hot, sweet, nasty words. He felt himself getting hard against her back, lifted himself to move on top of her. He eased her leg up over his shoulder, whispered more words. "Now talk to me," he said, "talk to me." She raised her head off the pillow, pressed her lips against his ear and whispered something he did not understand.

"Spanish," he said. "Say it in Spanish."

"I have to practice my English," she breathed.

"Not now," he said, going into her. "Later. Please. Make love to me in Spanish."

But only English words kept coming. For all he knew she was reciting a lesson she remembered from class. He started to go soft, felt his own heart slowing out of rhythm with what he was trying to do. Pilar was smiling at him.

"I can't do it in that language," he panted, collapsing on his back.

"What difference does it make?"

"I don't know. It just does. I never thought it would make a difference."

She rolled away from him and went back to sleep. She was teaching him a lesson, and though he wanted to get angry about it, his heart was too weighted to muster the fight. More upsetting than the lack of sex was how easily Pilar seemed to go without it. Sex was the only way he had ever been sure he was telling her how much he felt. It was his language for giving her joy. Now he saw that perhaps it had never meant that much to her after all.

🙟 🙟 🙟

On payday Antonio came into the machine shop to find a half-dozen of his co-workers huddled around Miguel's workstation, talking about the upcoming lay-offs.

"That rumor's been going around for a while," Antonio said.

"Today," Miguel said. "We're talking about today. They tried to keep it from us until the end of the day, but I saw the pink slips on Martínez' desk."

"Are you sure?" Gómez said.

"I'm pretty sure."

"Pretty sure?" someone else said. "Either you're sure or you're not. Which is it?"

"Calm down," Antonio said. "Tell me, Miguel, did you see any names?"

"No," he said, "but there was a stack of them."

One of the managers came to the door of the second floor office. Everyone looked up, then started to break apart.

Antonio put on his goggles and went back to his machine. He was losing his wife and now he was losing his job, and he had made no more progress on the business. Everything, everything was slipping away at a rate he couldn't seem to counter.

He turned his lathe back on, letting the hum of the machine calm him. He had always found something soothing about machines. Something about the predictability of them, he supposed.

At lunch he found Miguel out by the lunch truck. "I'm breaking away," he said. "I'm quitting. No one's going to fire me from a job. I've been here the least time, so I'm sure to be the first to go."

"Then we'll quit together," Miguel said.

"Are you sure about this?" Antonio said.

"I told you, I'm behind you completely. Anyway, it might save one of these other poor bastards' jobs. Let's get it over with."

On their way up the steps to the office, Antonio wanted more than anything else to call Pilar. He had never made a decision like this before without talking to her, and now he ached to hear her approving voice. Yes, she would approve, he was sure of it . . . . But just to hear her voice, just to hear her voice . . .

❀ ❀ ❀

On his first day working for Antonio, Miguel worked all afternoon with him in the hot sun clearing space for scrap piles in the two-acre dirt yard that Antonio had rented for his business. They took Antonio's GMC roll-off unit out for a drive so Miguel could get the feel of it, then came back to the yard to weld the drop-off containers they would need for pick-ups. It felt good to Antonio to work with his whole body, even though the work was tiring. But he still only had two regular customers: small machine shops in the south part of Hayward.

"Stop moping," Miguel said. "You have to have more faith. You're doing the right thing. I can feel it in my bones."

When that failed to cheer him up, Miguel disappeared behind one of the drop-off units, then casually reappeared wearing two aluminum oil funnels taped together like a bra as he went back to work. Antonio stared for a moment, then dropped to his knees in a fit of laughter.

*Ღ *Ღ *Ღ

At the lumber yard a few days later Antonio saw Rivera, his old English teacher, loading pine beams into the bed of a Ford pick-up. Antonio spun around to avoid him and went into the building with his head down, pretending not to notice him. But standing in line at the register he felt a hand settle on his shoulder.

"Antonio?" the voice said. "How's everything?"

"Oh, fine, fine," Antonio said. "Just picking up a few things for my new business."

"I didn't know you had your own business."

"I just started it a few months ago."

"That's wonderful. I've always wanted to do something like that."

He gave Antonio a friendly smile. Antonio laughed.

"What's so funny?"

"I thought you were going to test me on my English or something."

Rivera laughed too. "Listen," he said. "You left in such a hurry that last day, I never got a chance to tell you how much I enjoyed having you in my class."

Antonio stared at him. "Really?" he said.

"Yes, of course. I've seen very few students put so much effort into my class. And that wife of yours. What a talent. You're a very lucky man."

He shook Antonio's hand, then left him there, speechless. How wrong he had been to misjudge this man, to have made such an issue out of nothing. Certainly he had looked at Pilar with desire, but what man could have helped doing so? Antonio wished he were a stronger man, more deserving of Pilar. But she was the strong one, he knew, strong for being able to put up with his foolishness. Pilar, the pillar. Pilar, his support.

The dark period between them had gone on long enough. He saw what he had to do, while he had the courage to do it: shake off his jealousy and pride, and cast them away and never let them near him again. He would find a way to make things up to her.

So that night, awkwardly, wordlessly, he held out his hand to her in the manner of a gallant requesting a dance. She was scrubbing the bathroom tub at the time, yellow rubber gloves rising above her elbows.

"Please don't fool with me, Antonio."

"I want to take you out tonight."

"I have work to do."

"I'll do it for you later."

"And leave me with more work than if I'd done it myself? Dinner is almost ready. Go and change out of those overalls."

"Save it for tomorrow."

"It won't be as good tomorrow."

He kept his hand out. She kept scrubbing. Finally, she tossed the sponge down, peeled off the gloves. "There's that movie at the Bal. I guess we could go to that together. After we eat."

✿ ✿ ✿

It was an opening of a new movie with Olivia Rodríguez that had been playing in Mexico for several months, one that the papers were calling her comeback film after a two-year battle with alcohol. As they waited in line, a woman stopped to ask them something in English. Antonio wasn't sure if she was asking directions or what time the movie started, but Pilar answered her right away, in English. The woman asked something else, and again Pilar answered without hesitating. Soon they were deep in the thread of a conversation of which Antonio understood little.

There should have been nothing surprising about this. Pilar had always been fast to understand and had been practicing English daily with one of the neighbors. Only now did Antonio start to see what his wife's talent might mean for him.

Throughout the movie he could not stop thinking about it. He had always thought of the business as his. He had never thought of including Pilar in it, in part because she had never shown an interest, but really because, well, he had never thought of it. But now he saw that she was the one with the talent to help him make it take off. She was the one who could get him the English-speaking clients.

He didn't bring it up right away. He could only imagine Pilar's reaction. Is that what you were buttering me up for, Antonio? Yet another favor, another sacrifice of my time, to be your secretary?

He said nothing about it on the way home, nothing that night. Not until the next morning, after hours in bed crafting his words to sound as unconcerned as possible did he work his way around to the subject.

"Do you have a lot planned today?" he said.

"Housework. Errands. The usual. Why?"

"I was thinking, I'd like to bring you to see the yard sometime. It looks different since the last time you were there."

"Maybe some weekend," she said. "I have a lot to do."

"It must get tiring for you, the same thing every day."

She shrugged. "What's one to do? I can't complain."

"You could always come work for me." He laughed to make it sound like a joke.

"I can see it: me breaking my back at the scrap piles."

"I meant in the office. The phone, paperwork."

She started folding towels on the bed.

"I just thought it would be better than sitting around here all day."

"Is that what you think I do? Sit around the house all day?"

"No, no, no, that's not what I meant. Never mind, I don't know where that idea came from."

Pilar stacked the towels and carried them out to the bathroom. A couple minutes later she came back. "Who would take care of the housework?"

"We both could, on the weekends."

"And if you're working on the weekend?"

"Then it will have to go undone."

"And the neighbor's kid?"

"You've been doing that long enough."

She left the room again. The house was quiet. When Antonio had finished dressing, he came into the kitchen. Pilar was packing two lunch bags. "Let's get going," she said.

"Are you sure?"

She shrugged. "Anything to get out of scrubbing the floors for a day."

🐬 🐬 🐬

At the yard he showed her into the trailer office at the back. With arms folded she looked over the wood plank desk, the rusted file cabinets. She picked through a tangle of receipts on the desk

"All you'd have to do is answer the phones and do the scheduling," he said.

She ran her finger along the aluminum window sill. Finally she sat down and spread her hands flat on the desktop. "Well, what are we going to call it?" she said.

He stared at her.

"The business. It has to have a name, doesn't it? Otherwise what am I going to say when I answer the phone? 'Hi, this is Pilar, what the hell do you want?'"

He left her emptying the filing cabinets. "This is no way to organize any-thing," she said. "Give me an hour and I'll have a system set up for you."

Two hours later, she was on the phone with the yellow pages spread open in front of her. She held out two slips of paper to him. "Two new accounts," she said. "I've been on the phone all day calling all the machine shops. Ace through Zúñiga. I'm almost done. Tomorrow I'll start on welding and steel forming. Then I thought we could do our first mailing at the end of the month as a reminder."

"*Oye, hombre,*" Miguel said, after Antonio had introduced him to Pilar. "I had no idea you had such a good-looking wife. I can't believe how she's pulling things together around here. Forget what I said about cheating on her. This one is too good to risk."

That night Antonio awoke at two to find Pilar gone from bed. He found her sitting on the living room floor with green and white receipt pages spread out all around her.

"I couldn't sleep," she said, pushing up her reading glasses. "There's a fifty-dollar error on the books and it's been driving me crazy. I have to find it."

"Please, come to bed," he said. "You're working too hard."

"You want this business to be a success, don't you?"

"I don't want you to start hating it."

"Please, Antonio. This is the first interesting thing I've had to do in years. Can't you see how much I'm enjoying it?" She took off her glasses, entwined an arm around his leg and kissed his kneecap.

"All right," he said. "But please don't overdo it."

They worked together for the next five weeks. It amazed Antonio how smooth her face had become, eased of the lines of daily frustration. Antonio often lingered around the office, pretending to be busy just so he could look at her. She was in love with her work, and for the first time in their marriage, Antonio felt that he had actually given her something she valued. They still had not resumed making love, in any language, but they had at last reached an easy truce at home. And Antonio was not so foolish as to tamper with that.

❧ ❧ ❧

Just before Thanksgiving, Pilar showed him the account books for the work they had done over the summer. They had made a profit for two out of three months. "We can probably start paying Miguel a little more," she said.

"I was planning on it," Antonio said. "Starting the first of the year." He moved to give her a kiss. "Really, Pilar, thank you. There's no way I could have come this far without you. We should have a real Thanksgiving this year. We have reason to celebrate."

"Be sure to invite Miguel," she said. "We owe a lot to him, too."

"I wouldn't dream of doing this without him," Antonio said.

On Thanksgiving Eve, the three of them walked down the grocery store aisles together, Antonio filling the cart with the most expensive items he came across, and Pilar saying over and over, "No, Antonio, that's far too much food for just three people."

Miguel laughed as the two of them played tug-of-war with a frozen twenty-pound turkey. The apartment started to warm early the next day with the smells of the Thanksgiving meal.

Miguel arrived stuffed into a suit with wide, outdated lapels.

"Be careful you don't bend over," Antonio said. "That thing looks like it's about to rip down the seam."

"Don't laugh at me," Miguel said. "I wanted to add a little class to this gathering. But I think it must have shrunk since I last wore it."

They started with wine before dinner, the three of them finishing a full bottle while standing in the kitchen. Miguel told one joke after another, each a little dirtier than the last. How long had it been since Antonio had heard Pilar laugh this way, without restraint? Since he had seen her look happy? Maybe things were becoming good between them once again.

After the long meal, Antonio brought desserts out from the kitchen.

"Let's wait," Pilar said, crinkling up her nose. "I couldn't stand another mouthful."

But Antonio insisted that everyone try at least a bite of each kind of pie, since he had helped make them. Pilar tried to get up to start cleaning, but Antonio wouldn't let her. "More wine for everyone," he said, tearing the lead foil off a new bottle.

Miguel started into another story, this time about how he had once been with a woman when her husband came home, and he had had to step out onto the tenth-floor building ledge outside the bedroom to hide. "The neighbors started pointing. They thought I was trying to kill myself, so they called the police. They brought out a net for me to jump into."

The three of them laughed, Pilar hardest of all. She put her hand on Miguel's shoulder as if to keep from falling over. Her hand rested there.

Antonio went quiet, as if all the liquor had just drained out of him. He went to the kitchen for a glass of water. From there he could hear Pilar and

Miguel's high-spirited chatter, the playful clinking of glasses, hands drumming the table with hilarity. From the doorway he watched them.

A gray light fell over the apartment towards evening. Antonio took the far end of the couch and turned on the football game, but only stared at the set without really watching it. He had never learned the rules of the game, and the scurried movement of the players around the field only stirred his thoughts into greater disorder.

In the kitchen Pilar began putting away plates. From the dining table, Miguel was staring at her, his red eyes traveling up and down the course of her figure as she reached on tiptoes for the higher shelves. Antonio saw her look over her shoulder from the sink and smile at Miguel.

Miguel came over to the couch. "How's the game?" he said.

Antonio stood up and said he wasn't feeling well and went to lie down. He didn't get up again. He could feel himself slipping under the influence of another dark spell of jealousy, and knew better than to trust his own actions when he'd been drinking. Don't start tipping boats, he told himself, forget about it until morning.

🙦 🙦 🙦

Back at the yard on Monday, Antonio could not help noticing how Miguel kept looking at Pilar when he came into the office to check the schedule and drop off invoices. His gaze lingered over the curve of her frame as she talked on the phone or leaned into the open filing cabinet. How stupid Antonio had been to let this happen. Had he been so busy that he could not have seen it coming? He was dense. How could he have forgotten that Miguel was the biggest abuser of women he had ever known?

Antonio began sticking close to Miguel around the yard, began giving him the pick-ups that were the farthest away and took the longest to get to. Anything that needed to be done in the office, Antonio did himself. He could no longer laugh at Miguel's antics. By the end of the day, Antonio was too brimming with self-disgust to face Pilar.

That night, exhausted from his own thoughts, he lay next to Pilar, desperately wanting to hold her again, to assure himself that she was still his. But it would be a mistake to touch her. Any hint of rejection would balloon in his mind into something he did not want to believe. Throughout the night, jealously and loneliness alternated their visits to him, keeping him from sleep.

At work the next day, his temper finally flared when Miguel locked his keys in the GMC for the third time that week. "Goddamn you, you idiot, the amount of time we waste because of your stupid mistakes. . ." Acid rose in his throat, hot and bitter. He walked away without finishing his sentence.

For the rest of the day, he avoided Miguel at every turn. Every joke Miguel told seemed to have a double meaning. Every movement was an advance towards Pilar.

The next day, Miguel stood staring at him, with mouth slightly agape as Antonio rambled off his vague list of reasons for letting him go. Pilar had shown signs of a flu and Antonio had insisted she stay home for the day.

"I don't understand," Miguel said. "The business is doing so well."

"That was before we considered taxes," Antonio mumbled. "Sometimes these things happen. I can only say that it's a decision made with the business in mind. I'll be happy to give you two weeks pay."

Miguel looked at him as though he were peering into a dark, deep closet. Antonio hated his idiotic expression, his sloppy, overgrown shrub of a mustache.

"I wish I could explain in more detail," Antonio said.

"What have I done wrong?"

"Nothing," he said. "Now I've got some phone calls to make." He shuffled some papers, but Miguel did not move. Finally, Antonio had to leave the office. He left Miguel standing there, staring blankly at the place where Antonio had been sitting.

When he got home that night, he did not have time to unhook his overalls before Pilar flew at him.

"How could you, Antonio? What were you thinking? Don't you know he has alimony payments to make?"

He started to give her the same excuses he had given Miguel, but her words tore through his, shredding them to nothing. "Didn't you think to talk to me about this? What in the world were you thinking, Antonio?"

"We don't need him," he said.

"You can barely handle the customers you have."

"We need to think about saving money."

"We have plenty of money."

"It's already done." He tried to control his tone, but it was already slipping out of his control. Pilar blocked the doorway as he tried to leave the room.

"You're going to answer me. Tell me why you fired him. Something happened between the two of you. What was it?"

"It was a business decision."

"It wasn't a business decision."

"Why are you so upset?"

"He was our friend, Antonio."

"He was a dirty-mouthed abuser of women."

"He was with us from the beginning."

"Then maybe you'd like to go to him."

Why was it, he wondered, that words, when he most wanted them, were nowhere at hand. And why, when silence was his wisest option, did words fly recklessly from his lips with a life of their own?

"So that's it," said Pilar calmly. "That's what this is all about. You got some stupid notion in your head about the two of us and you went and fired him. Well, I hope you're satisfied."

"Can't I make a business decision without consulting you? It's *my* business, after all."

She held him with a hard, colorless gaze. Then she went into the bedroom and slammed the door.

❧ ❧ ❧

The next day she told him she was going back to Tijuana to stay with her parents. "Until I figure out what I want," she said. She was in the bedroom packing her suitcases.

"You're not going anywhere," Antonio said, but his words had no force. It was a half-uttered question, not a statement. "I'm not going to let you divorce me."

"I didn't say I wanted a divorce."

"What do you want?"

"I don't know. I want time to think."

"Just because of this? Pilar, it's nothing we haven't been through before."

She turned to him, stopping everything she was doing. "Yes, Antonio. And how many times should I be expected to go through it again?"

"Things were good between us again," he said.

She shook her head sadly and laughed. "Where have you been, Antonio? Things haven't been good between us for a long time. We haven't slept together in months. The only thing we shared was working on the business—excuse me—*your* business."

Before Pilar was to leave, Antonio went out of the house and started walking again. He did not want to be there when her friend Monica came to pick her up, did not trust his own actions. He walked because walking dispersed his thoughts enough to keep him sane from one moment to the next. He walked because he could think of nothing else to do. How had this happened, he thought. How could he have let it? He was losing her just when he was learning how to love her the way she wanted to be loved. He had been losing her for such a long time, the losing was out of his control, how could he have not seen it? He tried to get angry, if only to feel something different than this cold, spinning hollowness. But fear held him tight, the voice of it hovering close, spitting dark words in his ear. Now is the time to be afraid, it said. Later will be the time for regret.

He decided to go to the yard and work for the rest of the day, even though it was a weekend. It was the only place he could think to go, the only place he might be able to forget for a while. But when he opened up the office to get the keys to start up the crane, Pilar's lingering presence beared down on him.

The room smelled of the flowered air freshener she had brought in. Looking for the keys, he came across the neat stacks of billing statements that Pilar had been preparing on Friday. He sat down and paged through them, but didn't know what needed to be done. A different kind of fear swept over him, wrapped its arms around him. Not the pale, achy fear of losing love, but the sharp, pressing practical fear of losing all he had built. Pilar, the pillar. Pilar, his support. How had he let this happen? How had she become the linch-pin to everything that mattered to him?

He went out into the yard to work the crane. Here, for the last few months at least, he had had some happiness. But because it was Saturday, there was no noise coming from the steel forming company next door, no shouting from the construction site across the street. The silence was a canvas on which his mind could paint terrible pictures, write terrible words. To break the silence he turned on the generator and swung the Ohio magnet out over the scrap iron piles to move them into the containers. The loud crashing of steel against steel helped mash down the panic, broke up the fear.

Towards evening, the flat, gray winter light began slipping from the yard. Antonio climbed down from the crane and switched on the yard lights, flooding the yard in white, bringing up shadows in strange places. The electricity hummed, crackled. He went back to working the crane, the long arm of it sweeping back and forth from pile to container, container to pile. Long into the night the loud crashing went on, the crashing that obliterated thought, that obliterated the words that were going through his head, which was the language of love, which was the language more difficult to learn than any other.

CARRYING SERGEI

WHEN I WAS FOURTEEN, my parents made their living selling six varieties of tamales, the best ones in town, at the edge of the tourist district on the Avenida Revolución. My job before every sunrise was to spread the dough and tie the corn husks while my mother cleaned the leaves. I gave my work my full attention, measuring out equal portions of dough and shaping the tamales into neat, plump oblongs. I always worked in a room by myself. My family and I got along better that way.

On the morning I was to meet Sergei Mikhailovich before school, I only wanted to finish as quickly as I could. Sergei had bet me 2000 pesos that he could beat me in a race up Obregón Hill, and I was eager to collect my winnings. Sergei was new to Tijuana and could not have known that I was the only girl in the sixth grade who could scale all 364 steps by twos without stopping.

On the other side of the curtain that separated us, my mother's voice rose to a screech. "Get in there and help your sister. You're a big girl now. You're old enough to be of some use."

"Keep her out of my way," I yelled. "I'm in a hurry. I'll make her cry. I mean it."

"Everyone in this family can be of use," Mamá said.

"She's barely seven," I said.

"When you were seven, you did everything."

"I was exceptional."

"Exceptional girls don't talk back to their mothers. They don't start arguments with all the neighborhood."

"*Señora* Pacheco called me a thief. I had to defend myself."

"You didn't have to kick over her *tomatillos*. You didn't have to call her a *bruja vieja*."

I was on the verge of shouting, but I caught myself. My parents had allowed me to take a year off from school to help with the family business, but now that I was back in school, I seemed to be getting into arguments daily. Benita Rubio had told me how humiliating it was for her to be seen with someone who was always shouting, even in ordinary conversation. For a week I had been trying to break myself of the habit.

A few minutes later, Mamá tried to drag Alicia through the doorway, but Alicia grabbed the doorframe with both hands. "I'm giving you one last chance," Mamá said.

"Or else what?" I said, thumping out a mound of dough. "I've told you before, if you want her to obey, you have to threaten her."

Alicia lost her grip. She grabbed the curtain instead, pulling down the curtain and rod with a crash. I stood up and she squealed as I lifted her with one hand onto the stool next to mine.

"Put the tamales in boxes. Don't play with them. Be quiet."

When I had finished the last dozen tamales, I took off my apron and wiped my hands. I quietly plucked the daily sales ledger from the shelf above the stove and thumbed through the month's figures. I wasn't allowed to touch it, but Mamá often miscalculated, and I liked to check the totals for accuracy. Sure enough, I caught a mistake on the first glance. It was a wonder my father agreed to let her run the business while he was out of town. Her voice was too puny to attract customers above the horn-blaring downtown clamor, she often counted out change wrong, and she made the tamales twice as big as they had to be to appeal to the tourists. For a year I had been suggesting that we make them in two sizes, one for regular customers, and a smaller size for the Americans, who were always grinning as if there were nothing but bargains to be found in Tijuana.

I fixed the mistake, then leaned the ledger against the coupon jar at the same tilt I had found it.

"Did you finish your letter to Papá?" she said from the other room.

"I have to go," I said, reaching for my books on the stove burner. She came in, arms heaped to the chin with husks. She had gotten some of the silky yellow fibers in her hair. I went over and started to pick them out for her. She never looked in a mirror, and often went out into public with a dab of dough on her cheek or an earring missing from one ear. I got all the fibers out, but there was nothing I could do about her wispy drifts of hair.

On the way out I said, "Did you know you look very pretty?"

From the sink she looked over her shoulder at me as if a stranger had wandered into her kitchen.

"Benita thinks so too," I said.

"Thank you, Margarita. That's a fine compliment."

I back-stepped, one foot out the door.

"I'll bet if you pulled your hair out of your face, and tied it back. . ."

"Margarita! Did you finish your letter to Papá or not?"

"If you just bought some ribbon. . ."

"Do you want me to read it for you?"

"I already mailed it."

"I didn't give you a stamp."

"I got one from Benita."

"I thought you hated Benita."

"What?" I said, but I was already halfway out the yard.

"You hate Benita Rubio!"

I bounded over the slumped diamond link fence, scaring up the chickens in the neighbor's back yard. I didn't think I was asking much of my mother, only that she not be the untidiest woman in our district. Any day now my father was going to write for us to join him in Sacramento, California, where he was setting up a food-distributing business with my *Tío* Ramón, who was already a U.S. citizen. As much as my insides tightened at the thought of moving to a place with such a harsh sounding name, I hoped we could at least do it without drawing attention to ourselves.

Not drawing attention to myself was something I was becoming an expert at. Over the last year I had burst out of my girlish proportions, gaining inches over my classmates in height and in the breadth of my shoulders. I had packed onto my frame a new density of flesh that left speechless the relatives who hadn't seen me recently. Girls like me, my teacher told me over and over, were prone to attract attention, which explained why I was always getting into fights. I needed to take extra care to speak softly, move cautiously, and use my smile to distract upward. As I made my way through neighbors' back yards, I was careful not to raise too much dust. I took figs only from the trees of houses where I knew no one was home.

At Benita's house I went around to the front and tapped at the screen.

Her mother appeared, strangling a broom handle with both hands. "Benita doesn't want anything to do with you," she said.

"Good morning, *Señora* Rubio," I said, giving the slightest curtsey. Though Benita and I spent more time being enemies than friends, I had always liked her mother's enchanting eyes.

She turned sharply and I went in. I looked around the room at her mother's paintings of French landscapes and hand-embroidered sofa covers. I wished that some day we would have such nice things, but Papá said the next few years were going to be full of sacrifices. I had only the bleakest picture of life in Sacramento. Benita told horrible stories about her second cousin Luz, who had been cheated out of her savings by an American who had promised to marry her. She had become a maid in Anaheim and had had to travel by bus two hours each morning to clean a ten-room house where only one person lived. She had finally killed herself, Benita said, by locking herself in one of four bathrooms and mixing together in a sink all the most toxic cleaning chemicals she could find.

Benita bulleted out of her own room on a direct course for the door. "You can walk with me if you want, but don't expect me to be pleasant." The screen slammed behind her.

I caught up with her down the block. "I need you to time the race for me today. I think I can beat my old record."

Benita swung her books close to her side in swift, angry jerks, eyes straight ahead. Her polished black shoes flashed sharply in the sun with each step.

"Can I carry your books for you?" I reached for them, but she pinched them more tightly under her arm.

A few moments passed. Then she blurted out, "I never thought I would be caught cheating."

"You were supposed to miss two or three problems on purpose," I said. "Everyone knows you're not smart enough to get the same score as me in science."

"I'm not stupid," Benita said.

"In some things, you are very stupid."

"You're going to kill yourself on those steps."

"I have excellent balance."

"Look at what happened to Rico Candelario."

"He was blind in one eye."

"My mother says to have nothing to do with you."

"A lot of mothers say that."

After a few minutes, I added, "I'll give you a quarter of the money I win. Five hundred pesos."

"We'll see," she said. "It depends."

"Seven-fifty," I pressed.

"I said it depends."

What it depended on, I knew, was whether Marisol Cruz and Gloria Rivera were already at school or not. These were the girls that had recently made room for Benita in their privileged and dangerous circle, taking her with them to their meeting place along the ocean and giving her cigarettes to smoke. With their rich, tempestuous hair and eyes that looked on everything with smoldering disdain, they were beyond popularity, as if that were a childish stage they had abandoned long before they had ever cracked their first pack of cigarettes. Benita was careful not to spend too much time with me when they had her in sight.

After a few minutes, she slowed her pace and sighed. "I suppose I should be tolerant of you. After all, when you leave, life for you isn't going to be easy."

"You don't know how it is," I said, faking enthusiasm. "Life in Sacramento is going to be fantastic. I'm going to have whatever I want."

For the rest of the way, I tried to copy her dainty, turned-in steps, the way she smiled at people she didn't know. When we passed Alfredo Zúñiga's house, she smiled and giggled to him on the porch. I did the same after her. I angled my books against my side the way she did. I swung my hips in the same rhythm.

I felt ridiculous. I sprinted out in front of her through the Colonia General Estrada. I took a leap at a limb of the peach tree, threaded my legs up through my arms like a gymnast, and swung upside-down until she caught up with me.

The Obregón school came into view on the distant hill that shot up at the downtown's western edge. It was a grim, looming, two-story building that looked more like a penitentiary than a public school. I was back for my final year, older than my classmates and a half foot taller than any teacher. Rules and restrictions and teachers' threats no longer intimidated me. As long as I kept to myself, both students and teachers left me alone.

But the most important thing I had conquered didn't lie inside its walls and corridors. It was the steep concrete steps that rose hazardously an eighth of a mile up the hill. Fifty-two broad steps lead to the first plateau, then another fifty-two to the next, and so on all the way to the smog-hazy summit. I had raced these steps hundreds of times, and my growth spurt of the last year had pushed me to the top rank of racers. But because of my new effort to stand out less, I only raced if money was involved.

Benita stopped, scanned the top of the hill before we moved forward.

I nearly split open with laughter when I saw my opponent squatting on the bottom step. Sergei's thumbs were hooked into the enormous side pockets of adult-sized work pants that were bunched and cinched at his waist with rope. They were held together with so many different-colored patches that you couldn't tell where the pants began and the patches ended. He wore shoes with no socks, and his arms, skinny as curtain rails, jutted out of a shirt that was secured with every variety of button and even a safety pin where the collar button should have been. I was raised better than to laugh at the poor, but I wasn't laughing at him because he was poor. I was laughing because there was no way this humped, scrubby boy in clumsy clown clothes and hard-soled shoes had a chance to win against me.

"Did you bring the money?" I said. He smiled up at me and nodded. The few times I had heard him speak, it was with an accent, the words gurgling in his throat like gravel swirling in a sink drain. His family had moved here from Russia under circumstances *Profesora* Ruiz had never been able to get him to talk about. She had tried to get us to draw him out with questions about Russia, but people had just stared at him. General interest in him had lasted about three minutes.

I started doing body-twists to get limber.

"You'd better warm up," I said. "You don't want to tear a ligament."

He jumped up awkwardly like a broken stick puppet, started doing side-twists as well. I started doing deep-knee bends. He did deep-knee bends. I started running in place. So did he.

"Stop it," I said. "You can't do everything I do."

He stuck his hands back in his pockets, grinned at me stupidly. I sighed, shook my head. He had no idea how I was about to humiliate him.

"All right," I said. "Let's get started."

Benita took out her expensive watch with the built-in stopwatch that she was always showing off and started zigzagging up the hill. She was hardly recognizable when she got to the top. Marisol and Gloria must have been nowhere in sight, because she started yelling through cupped hands: "Attention, attention! Gather around, students of the Obregón School for the race of the century. Margarita Navarrete will race the insidious communist in a contest for world supremacy. It's the event you don't want to miss!"

I didn't know what a communist was or what insidious meant, but I appreciated her ability to stir up a crowd. If you were going to humiliate someone, the humiliation might as well be public and therefore complete.

I put my right foot on the bottom step. Sergei did the same.

Benita raised her hand. "Four. Three. Two. One. . ."

We launched up the steps before she said "go." I took the first set of them at an easy pace, letting the blood fill my legs. I let Sergei stay a few steps ahead of me. I let my mind unravel, threads of thought reaching out and touching whatever they wanted to. Then, slowly, I started to pull them in.

I started taking the steps by twos. I brought my breathing into rhythm with my legs, two strides for every breath in, two for every breath out. The cold air was like a knife stabbing into my lungs, but I didn't fight it. When I saw Sergei's footing start to get sloppy, I pulled my mind down into myself. At the third tier I shot up from behind and passed him.

By the fourth tier, the throbbing in my heart was like a fist punching the inside of my chest. The ache in my legs was fire burning up the wicks of my muscle fibers. The pain, I remembered, was not my opponent. I got down into the empty center that the pain seemed to come from. In a final white burst that had nothing to do with physiology, I exploded up the last steps to the top.

The group at the top of the hill was bigger than I had guessed.

"You did it," Benita said. "You beat your own time by four seconds."

I threw my arms overhead like a prizefighter. I kicked dirt up from the pavement. I whooped and hollered and jumped from foot to foot.

Sergei straggled up the steps a half-minute later, a gasping, perspiring, heaving jumble of bones and rags and patches. He had given up somewhere on the fourth incline, and was still pumping air too hard to speak. He didn't seem to notice kids laughing at him. He just stood there, puffing and sweating and smiling.

Smiling. I couldn't believe it. I had won by the biggest margin ever and he didn't seem to realize it. I repeated my victory dance. I whooped even louder. "You lost!" I said.

He kept smiling at me stupidly.

"I said, you lost! You're the loser. Are you stupid? Don't you understand?"

That smile was the most maddening thing I had ever seen. Crooked, translucent teeth, like pieces of broken eggshell, fought each other for space in the mosaic of his grin. He didn't try to insult my size or accuse me of cheating like boys usually did when they lost. He was being what no other boy I had raced had ever been. A good sport. And it was making me furious.

"Say something," I said. "Don't just stand there."

The school bell rang out furiously. Kids began ambling off, but I didn't move. I gazed hard at Sergei's dusty walnut hair, at the rings of pasty dirt around his neck. I didn't care if I got yelled at for being late. I was going to wring some satisfaction out of my victory. I was going to make him act like the loser he was.

I held his eye until I finally saw his smile quake. How stupid he was, I thought, to stand there with his back to the steps. If I were to shove him he would have nothing to hold onto. I wouldn't even have to shove that hard, just give a slight push, a tap on the shoulder. . .

I don't know why I did it. It was hardly a push at all, just the merest brushing of my palm against his protruding collarbone, as if I were brushing away a piece lint. But it was enough to tip him backwards, skinny arms helplessly rotating out at his sides, eyes peeling as he slowly but completely lost balance and fell, like a leaf from a tree arching backwards over itself in slow, continuous motion, until he lay in silence near the bottom of the top tier.

I ran to the front of the school and grabbed *Profesora* Ruiz. She must have seen in my face that something was wrong, for she immediately began to run in the direction I had come from. She plunged down the steps towards Sergei, hips bouncing, heavy wool dress swirling about her legs.

Sergei lay thirty steps down, like a pile of colorful laundry. I couldn't see his face. I couldn't tell his arms from his legs. I started to say something, but the whiteness of *Profesora* Ruiz's face when she looked up struck the words out of me. A light drizzle started. She threw her keys up to me and told me to unlock the class and tell the other students to wait for her there.

In the class the chatter of students filled the air, but from my seat in the back right corner, everything sounded muffled as if through glass. Benita and Marisol and Gloria had pushed their desks together and were huddled close in gossip. No one seemed to notice that anything was wrong, although Sergei's empty seat in the center of the room was to me like the gaping eye of a whirlpool that I was fighting not be sucked down into for the thing I had done.

Lies started to fill my head. I hadn't pushed him. He had slipped. We had been wrestling. He had been showing off. I hadn't seen anything. It was his word against mine.

I knew I would never be able to repeat one convincingly, but they kept filling my head like water rushing into a sinking boat. I was going down in a whirl of wretchedness and guilt and fear, the whole room spinning around me with not so much as a fiber of hope to grasp.

It seemed like an hour before the teacher came back, pale and spent, wringing a handkerchief on which I was sure I saw blood. She said that an ambulance had taken Sergei to the Catholic hospital, but that he would be fine. When no one pressed her for more, she opened a notebook to read from, but her voice choked. She dismissed us, pulling the door open as she stepped out into the hall.

There was a rush for the door, but I didn't move. I gripped the sides of my desk. I waited for her interrogation.

Several minutes passed and she still hadn't come back into the room. I went to the door and looked out. There was no sign of her. There was no sign of anyone up or down the hall.

I stepped out quietly. I made my way slowly to the exit, my criminal's heart pounding. I stepped out into the light rain.

I ran. I ran down the steps, taking a dangerous six-step leap past the place where Sergei had fallen, down La Segunda to the bottom of the hill and past the banks and stores of the tourist district, then out into the wide, blank Bulevar Agua Caliente. I ran with a force I had never run with before, perilously fast across the slick pavement, the rain stinging my face, out to where the boulevard funneled into a dusty road beading with rain but not yet muddy. I ran with a speed that had nothing to do with trying to get somewhere and had everything to do with escaping my guilt, as if the earth were spinning nightmarishly fast beneath me.

The house was empty when I got home. It was still morning, but the clouds gave the room the weary feeling of late afternoon. I paced, rain and sweat sizzling down my face and arms, my skirt sticking to my legs. Consequences began to bear down on me. Benita's mother would forbid her from seeing me. She would tell the other mothers in the neighborhood and everyone would be talking. I would be kicked out of my school and sent to some other, terrible school in Tijuana where they still practiced corporal punishment. And that was if the police didn't get involved. The tragic lives of Benita's cousins would be nothing compared to what was going to happen to me.

I stopped pacing and tried to catch my breath. There was still the possibility that Sergei would say nothing. But the only way that seemed likely was if he were dead. And if I were to wish for such a thing, how could I ever live with myself?

The rain thudded louder and louder on the windows as the afternoon stretched on. I looked for chores to do to make the time go faster, but the dishes were washed, and the floor had been swept. When my mother came home, I could not bear to be in the same room with her. I skipped dinner and went to bed early.

I waited for sleep to take me away, but sleep would not come. Each time I was about to drift off, I would think I heard someone at the door talking to my mother and I would jolt awake.

Late into the night my sister stirred next to me as I got out of bed. In the kitchen I dug out a sheet of paper from one of the cabinets. Quickly, but firmly, I wrote,

Dear Papá,

I am writing to say that I am very excited about moving to the United States. I know I have complained in the past about not wanting to go, but I have changed a lot since you last saw me and I realize that moving is the best thing for us. I beg for you to send for us as soon as possible.

I would be more than happy to come ahead of Mamá and Alicia if you think I can be of use.

Love, your adoring daughter,
Margarita

The next morning Mamá said she was feeling ill and wanted me to take over for her downtown after I had finished in the kitchen. Getting out of school that day was like a small, brilliant miracle. I got a stamp from her, left the house early, and mailed my letter at the first mailbox I saw.

Downtown was especially crowded, with tourists thronging the sidewalks and cars blaring horns futilely in clogged traffic. At first I was glad for the distraction, but soon everywhere I thought I saw people looking at me. I found myself giving out incorrect change and getting yelled at by locals who thought I was trying to cheat them. Just after three o'clock a police car came screaming up the street. I held my breath and crouched behind the register until it passed. Another hour must have gone by before I noticed that someone had stolen over ten thousand pesos from the till. I closed the stand up early and made my way home, exhausted and on the verge of tears.

Mamá wasn't feeling any better the next day, and I was able to put off returning to school through the weekend. But by Sunday, my misery was unbearable. Benita, whom I might at least have confided in, had not come by once. My crime was now common knowledge.

The day I was to go back to school, I got my chores over with early. I thought about skipping school for a few more days, hoping that miraculously my father would write for me to join him before I got caught. But the thought of another day alone was worse than the thought of facing what was coming.

Leaving the house, I cleared my thoughts the way I did before a race. I went the long way around the neighborhood to avoid running into anyone I knew.

I was the first one to arrive on the school grounds. I locked myself in a stall in the girls' room on the north side of the building, listening to the chatter beginning to grow outside. A half hour later the bell screamed out. I waited until I didn't hear a voice. When I was sure all of the students were in their seats, I unlocked the stall. I made my entrance.

I went to my seat at the back of the class without looking at anyone. I could tell everyone was looking at me. *Profesora* Ruiz wasn't there yet.

Profesora Ruiz swept into the room. The door banged shut behind her, as if on my future. I put my head on my desk. I waited for her to address me.

"Let's begin today's class with a short science lesson," she began.

I peered over my forearms.

"Over the weekend did anyone hear about the satellite the Russians put into orbit around the earth?"

I lifted my head. I looked around. "What happened to Sergei?" I asked Raúl Diego, the sullen, fat-lipped boy to my left.

"I don't know, he fell down the steps. What do I care?"

"Has anyone said how he fell?"

"It was raining. The clumsy bastard slipped. He'll be back after Easter. What are you, in love with him or something?"

I leaned back in my seat. I breathed, as if from a fresh source of air.

The teacher weaved up and down the aisles as she continued to talk about the Soviet satellite called Sputnik. She said she wished Sergei were in class so that we could get his reaction to the news from his home country. She explained how an object, like the earth or the moon, stays in orbit by falling in such a way that it never reaches what it is falling towards. But mostly she talked about how we were witnessing an incredible time in the history of science, and about how it was important that we remember where we were when it happened, because it was a moment we would want to carry with us for the rest of our lives.

She continued to talk in a high pitched tone that sounded as much like fear as excitement. And I, still reeling from my narrow escape, had to agree with her: I would always remember this time in my life and that the world that we traveled on was nothing more and nothing less than a thing to be astonished by.

🙞 🙞 🙞

The next few days had the breezy lightness to them that comes after a storm has cleared through. By the time Easter vacation arrived, I had put Sergei out of my mind. I gladly got back to my routine of chores and trying to improve myself.

Benita had not come by my house for nearly two weeks. She had been all but ignoring me at school. When my mother told me one day that she had come by looking for me, I knew it had to be because the bottom had fallen out of her friendship with Marisol and Gloria. I decided to make her wait a few days before talking to her. But the next day an even better opportunity for revenge unfolded when I ran into Marisol and Gloria on my way through the Parque Teniente Guerrero.

Instead of pretending not to see them, I cut them off on the path. "I know where you can get cigarettes," I said. "For free. With no trouble."

They looked at each other with raised eyebrows. I turned and they started following me.

At my house I lead them down into the basement, where I remembered my father months ago had left two dozen cartons of his favorite cigarettes, Winston's.

The girls squatted down close to the dirt floor, ran their long, thin fingers over the dusty boxes. "What do you want for them?" Marisol said.

"Nothing," I said. "Just let me follow you for a couple of days. Let me spend some time with you. I'll stay out of your way. I just want to see where you spend your time on the beach."

Nothing would get under Benita's skin more than to see me going around with the very people who had dropped her.

Marisol whispered something in Gloria's ear. They looked at each other. They shrugged, nodded. "You can go around with us for a month if we can have all these," she said.

That same day I followed them through the hills towards the shore, where they showed me the hillside crevasse where they spent their hours smoking on weekends and after school.

"Nobody bothers us here." Gloria said. "We can do what we want. It doesn't matter that you've seen it. We move to a different place every few weeks."

It was a cool, overcast day, but they nevertheless flung off their blouses and laid back topless on their blankets, their hair spread out around them in the sand like starbursts. I was speechless with envy at how comfortably they did this, not even looking first to make sure we were alone. I thought they might ask me to do the same, but they never did, and I was glad.

I followed them around for the next few days, trying not to say anything embarrassing. To my surprise, they didn't seem to mind my being there as long as I didn't say anything when we ran into friends of theirs from other schools. I offered to carry their books and blankets for them, and brought left-over tamales from home. And every day on the way home, I made sure we lingered in front of Benita's house for a few minutes before moving on.

One day while we were wading ankle-deep in one of the foamy inlets, the subject of Sergei's accident came up.

"They say that he blinded himself," Gloria said.

"You're an idiot," Marisol said, splashing mud at her calves. "He'll be back in school in four weeks. If he were blind, he would have to go to a blind school."

"You're the idiot," Gloria hissed. "I didn't say I believed it, just that that's what people are saying."

"The fact is," Marisol went on, "that he had an arm amputated. And on top of that, he's suffering from amnesia. He doesn't even know who he is."

"I'm not sure I believe it," Gloria said, but only after a pause long enough to allow the image of a one-armed boy to root itself firmly in our minds.

I knew better than to listen to rumors, especially from these two, but for the rest of the day I couldn't help thinking again about what I had done. I needed the peace of mind of knowing that he wasn't too badly off, and I wasn't going to be able to wait four weeks to get it.

I remembered him telling *Profesora* Ruiz once that his family lived south of our school in the highest part of the Colonia Obregón. So on the first Monday of Easter vacation I crossed downtown in the direction of the highest hills in Tijuana.

The Calle Segunda twisted and turned up the hill for several miles. The further I rose, the further apart the wood and stucco houses became, with bougainvillea climbing up the sides of some of the porches and lemon and fig trees in the yards. I was getting tired and was about to turn back when I saw a house with a gate sheared off its hinges and overgrown with untrimmed sweet peas. Snapdragons and weeds rocketed up all around the property along a fence that was patched with knobless doors hammered up where planks had fallen away. Through a gap in the fence I saw a pair of patchwork pants swaying from a clothesline. I had found the place.

I didn't go up to the door. I only wanted to get a glimpse of Sergei. But I couldn't see any motion in the house.

I followed the fence down the side of the house to the back yard gate and peered through the slats. I heaved myself up onto the gate and with great balance quickly walked along the top of the back yard fence. I pulled myself up into the limbs of a tree in the corner of the yard. I worked my way up into the highest branches for a better view.

Loud chatter spilled from the open windows. Then, after about twenty minutes, the back door sprang open. Sergei hopped out on one foot, his leg in a cast that stretched from toe to thigh. He still had two arms. He carried a dirty yellow crutch, but he hardly relied on it, mostly just dragged it around with him as he clumped about the yard. I waited for him to go back in.

He didn't. Instead, appearing behind him was the largest woman I had ever seen, with shoulders that seemed to strain the seams of her dress and legs even sturdier than mine. Her arms were loaded with cast-iron platters of food and silverware, and a tablecloth was draped over her shoulder. She began to lay a meal out on the grass—right under the tree I was hiding in.

I watched them for several minutes, trying to identify the sweet, meaty smell that was rising from their plates into the tree. After a few minutes I tried to scoot along the limb to get more comfortable, but my skirt caught and I started to lose balance. I reached for a branch. The leaves rustled, sending a shower of blossoms onto the tablecloth they had spread out. They looked up.

I climbed down to the tree's base. His mother jumped to her feet, pulling Sergei close to her as she gasped something in low Russian. But Sergei's face was wrinkled with amusement, as if he had been in on the secret all along. He said something to her in Russian, which seemed to put her at ease. Then, she let out a loud "Ahhhhhhhhhhhh" and gave him a knowing wink.

Excuses were already whirling through my mind when she took me by the arm and handed me her plate. I looked at her.

"She wants you to eat," Sergei said. "Go ahead. There's plenty."

"I was just in the neighborhood," I said, "and I. . ."

She gestured aggressively at the food. I took a mouthful of fried potatoes, and she went into the house for another plate.

"Why didn't you say anything?" I whispered to Sergei. "Why didn't you tell anyone?"

He looked at me in surprise, then limped quickly into the house. I thought I should get out of there while I could, but he came back at once with his hand extended. In it was a cluster of hundred peso bills, the money he had lost in our bet.

"I don't want your dirty money," I said. "Don't you remember what happened? Don't you remember what I did?"

His eyes darted about. I wondered if it was true about the amnesia.

"Look," I said, "people at school were wondering about you, that's all. I thought I'd come and check to make sure you were all right. I'll see you in a couple of weeks."

"I won't be there for a month," he said. He rapped his knuckles proudly on his cast. "I can't climb the hill with this on."

"Oh. Well. Tell your mother thanks." I turned to go.

On my way to the gate his mother caught my arm and gave me a big-toothed smile even broader than Sergei's. "You come back. Tomorrow or after tomorrow. Sergei is by himself. You come back and see him?"

As I let gravity pull me back down the hill, I told myself I had nothing to be scared about anymore. I could stop worrying. Everything was back to normal.

A few days later, as I passed the street that lead to Sergei's neighborhood, I thought about how kind Sergei's mother had been, about how earnest her invitation to visit had been. It had been very rude of me to leave without finishing his mother's food or even saying goodbye. I had a bag of a dozen extra tamales that I had planned to heat up over a fire with Marisol and Gloria on the beach. I decided to take them to Sergei's mother instead. I didn't need yet another parent in Tijuana thinking I was unmannered and warning other parents against me. I turned up the hill.

This time I pushed the gate aside and knocked at the front of their house. In the living room, Sergei's mother threw up her hands and came to the door. Her figure was even larger than I had remembered, her enormous shoulders spanning the doorframe and her huge hands pressed flat on her hips. She lead me into the living room with much fuss, patting me vigorously on the back as she called up for Sergei.

"I just wanted to drop these off for you," I said, opening my bag. "It's my father's recipe, but I made them."

I looked around the room. From the center of the ceiling hovered an enormous chandelier with many of the glass pieces missing. The room was otherwise spare, but impressive, with a sofa and some throne-like chairs with faded cushions drooping over the sides. Through a door to the right I saw another room that looked just as spacious. In the middle of it, floating in a mist of sunlit dust, was a black lacquer piano.

Sergei must have seen me looking at it when he hopped down the stairs. He took my wrist and lead me towards it. I didn't like the idea of him touching me, but I had never known anyone with a chandelier or a piano, and I was curious to see what else they had.

In the piano room I walked around the edges of a dull red carpet, through shafts of warm sunlight, listening to my footsteps echo as if in a museum. At the far side of the room I came to a cabinet filled with plaques and awards. I tried to read the inscriptions, but I had never seen such an alphabet. I was about to ask him to tell me what they said when the room behind me exploded with music. I spun around, holding my breath at the hugeness of the sound. Sergei was sitting at the piano.

He was bent over the keys, leaning into them with the same intensity he showed in school when he was working on a test. The music was unlike anything I had ever heard before. The sound rolled out around him in great swells that swept away all thought. I came closer. His hands seemed to have a life of their own, long fingers dancing vigorously across the keys like angry, but elegant flesh-toned spiders. Then the flood ebbed, pulled into itself as if suddenly embarrassed by its own emotion, and receded to the faintest, saddest trickle of notes I had ever heard.

I stared at his slender back as if he were someone new to me. All at once he spun around on his stool, as if to catch on my face the expression he knew he had produced.

His mother swept in, again carrying plates, this time loaded high with steaming tamales. She set them on a low table by the window that faced the back yard and went out. She left the door open, but not wide open.

My head was racing. "You can play," I said. "And all these awards— they're yours. From Russia?"

He slid his cast under the table and started spearing tamales with his fork. Through a mouthful of food, he said that his father had also been a musician, a violinist. He had decided to get the family out of the country when the government insisted on separating Sergei from them to study in Moscow. His father's own career had been controlled by such state decisions, and he did not want his son's life manipulated in the same way, no matter how many favors government officials lavished on him. They convinced two long-time friends who were doctors to fake X-rays and test results showing that Sergei was dying from a brain disease that could only be cured in the West. Once he and his mother were out of the country, they went into hiding, first in Switzerland, then in France, taking two years to work their way to Tijuana, where many of their relatives had moved twenty years earlier. Only he and his mother had been allowed out. His father was still there.

"Why was it so hard to leave?" I asked.

"My father says that it makes the country look bad when people try to leave," he said. "Besides, they didn't want to lose a national treasure."

I looked at him blankly. It took me a few seconds to realize that he was talking about himself.

As he told me more about what his life as a performer had been like, I stared at him with my fork poised in my right hand. He had been playing piano since he was four and had even met the president of Russia. Electricity traveled in slow waves over my skin. I was sitting in a room with the most fascinating person I had ever met. I was sitting in a room with genius.

My food was cold by the time I tasted it. "You must really miss your country," I said. "You must miss the attention."

His head popped back in surprise. "This is my country," he said. "And I will be famous no matter where I go."

I jumped up to help his mother clear the plates a few minutes later, but she waved me away. "You come back, play with Sergei? Later this week?"

"Yes," I said, a little breathlessly. "I'll be back tomorrow."

*⟡⟡ *⟡⟡ *⟡⟡

When I arrived the next day I found the two of them in the back yard, trying to lift a stepping stone imbedded in the dirt in order to make room for a new garden.

"Let me help you with that," I called out. I squatted down and wedged my fingers under the stone. I dug in my heels, drove my legs up as hard as I could. In a few seconds it came loose.

Sergei's mother gave a gasp as I hoisted it onto my shoulder and moved it over by the fence. "Don't worry," I said. "I can lift a lot more than this." I got to work on the next stone, then the next. In a few minutes I had moved all fifteen of them.

Sergei applauded me, and his mother patted me on the back. She held me at arm's length. "You are a big girl," she said. "Big and good. Very strong."

It was the first time anyone had ever commented on my size without embarrassing me. As she went back to work in the dirt, I watched the muscles in her back moving under her tight dress. Here was a woman who, it occurred to me now, took large steps when she walked, who laughed and yelled loudly without covering her mouth, and who lifted and hoisted and moved as if these were the things her body was made for. She wore dresses of the most eye-catching green, and never a slimming pleat in any of them. I wondered for a moment if this were some kind of strange dream.

Inside we washed up, and afterwards Sergei played a piece for us that he had just learned, by someone named Tchaikovsky, whose name they made me try to pronounce, laughing all the while at my attempts. He followed this with two sad pieces called sonatas, one by someone named Prokofiev, another by

Rachmaninov. Then he closed the lid, refusing to go on, as if he believed that any more would lessen my appreciation of his talent.

I came by after school a couple more times that week, bringing extra tamales and *chicharrones* with me. We lounged in the huge chairs while eating, something my mother would never have let me do. I thought about asking Sergei to give me lessons, but when I looked at the size of my hands, I thought better of it.

Just before the end of the Easter vacation, a strange thing happened. I woke one morning feeling not quite like myself, and yet very much like myself, as if something in the world that had not been right before had suddenly shifted into its proper place. I found that I was no longer resenting things my mother said or mistakes she made or the way she dressed. And when my sister broke my favorite barrette, I had no urge to yell. But most strange of all was the fact that the things I had most been trying to change about myself—my awkwardness, my always getting into fights and arguments—seemed to have fixed themselves. I was lighter in body and mind, as if gravity had released me from the orbit of my old habits. I was flying through life like never before.

I was much more relaxed with Marisol and Gloria, as well. I stopped trying to do things that I thought would please them, and did not hesitate to tell them when I thought they were being nasty and childish. But in spite of their pettiness, I was beginning to enjoy the time I spent with them. They began to take my presence for granted, even came by the house looking for me a couple of times. But I didn't tell them about Sergei. His life carried an aura of secrecy to it that for some reason I felt it was my responsibility to protect.

The morning Sergei was to have his cast off, I was rushing out the back door when I nearly ran into Benita. Her face had the bruised look of a storm cloud waiting to burst.

"Where are you going?" she said.

I stuck my hands in my pockets, leaned casually against the corner of our outhouse. "Nowhere."

"I haven't seen you in a while," she mumbled at the ground.

"Yes, well. I've been busy downtown helping Mamá. And, of course, I've been spending a lot of time with Marisol, and, well, you know . . ." I started to go back in, but Benita loomed close. "They're saying you're in love with the Russian," she said.

I forced out a laugh. "That's crazy. Who told you that? But I'm not interested. Well, it was good to see you." I shut the door.

Through the curtains I watched her disappear. As soon as she was out of sight, I bolted for the Colonia Obregón.

I found Sergei reclined on the sofa with his foot up on a stack of encyclopedias. "You're not going to believe what people are saying," I said. "They're saying that you and I . . . that we've been . . . that we're sweethearts." The word echoed terribly in the big room. "How could something like this happen? We have to do something."

He smiled at me.

I swirled stormily about the room. "Don't you understand? Don't you see what this means?" Without using his crutch, he hopped to one foot and kissed me.

It was hardly a kiss at all, just a soundless brushing of his lips against mine. But the effect was devastating, like that suspended moment in slipping from a tree or roof when you realize how far you still have to go. Sergei Mikhailovich remembered exactly what I had done to him. But he hadn't cared. Because he had been in love with me all along. And Sergei Mikhailovich was in love with me now.

"I can't stay here," I said. "I never thought anything like this would happen." I was turning to go, when I realized that he was still wearing a cast. I stopped. "I thought you were supposed to get that off today."

I noticed for the first time how pale and tired he looked. "The bones didn't heal right," he said. "The doctor had to reset them."

"You mean . . ." I swallowed.

"They had to re-break the bones," he said weakly.

"What about school?" I said. "You can't afford to fall further behind."

He shrugged, as if that meant nothing to him, then sat down again. I stood for a long time, not knowing what to say. His eyes fluttered with exhaustion. After a few minutes, he drifted off to sleep.

❧ ❧ ❧

I made sure to meet Marisol and Gloria at the river on time the next day. I didn't care what they thought about me and Sergei, but they were the hub through which all gossip passed. They could demolish a rumor as easily as give life to one. The day was hot, and in rolled up pants we settled down by the shore. They didn't mention Sergei, but their curiosity hovered in the air with the persistence of summer insects. Then, as we were talking about how Rico Candelario had disfigured his face playing with gunpowder, Marisol casually lobbed the first grenade.

"Even so, he still isn't as ugly as, let's say, Sergei Mikhailovich."

I could almost hear their eyes click towards me in their sockets.

"I agree," Gloria said. "Or as dirty. They say he never bathes."

I gave them no reaction.

"You wouldn't know anything about that, would you, Margarita?"

I yawned, stretched my limbs out in the sun. "Actually," I said, "I've been to his house a few times."

They lifted their heads slightly off their blankets.

"Oh, yes," I said. "His mother buys tamales from my mother. But she has a bad back, so I often deliver directly to their house. She often invites me in. Did you know they have a beautiful piano?"

Their heads settled down again, the rumor dead.

❧ ❧ ❧

When I got home, Sergei was waiting for me, crutch in hand, on the front steps. In the late afternoon shade, his face shone pale with discomfort. It was nearly two miles from his house to mine.

"What are you doing here?" There was no harshness in my voice.

"Why haven't you come to see me?" he said.

Never before had he looked so thin, and his eyes were ringed with dark circles. He tried to say something else, but trembled on his crutch as if about to collapse. I reached out for him and caught him, eased him back onto the steps. When he had his strength back, I walked him home, stopping so that he could rest along the way. At his front door, he leaned against me. He smelled of cinnamon and chocolate. There was nothing dirty about him.

When I went by to check on him the next day at noon, he was looking brighter, nestled into the big sofa in the living room. He offered to play the piano for me, but I wouldn't let him get up. Instead he told me more about his plans to someday be a composer. That would come in time, I said. First, he had to recuperate so he could get back to school.

Over the next few weeks, we slipped back into our habit of seeing each other. I stopped spending time with Marisol and Gloria. His mother asked if I would mind helping her with the garden one or two days a week until Sergei was better. She wanted to start planting zinnias, she said, though it was long past the season for planting zinnias. I told her I would be more than happy to.

The rumors, of course, began to grow again. I could see it in the smirks of the kids I passed on the street in my neighborhood, in the fact that Marisol and Gloria stopped coming by my house looking for me. But in the comfort and warmth of Sergei's music-filled house these things seemed far away. I let myself sink into whatever each day presented.

One night, after spending nearly the entire day at Sergei's house, I lay in bed thinking about what I had fallen into. I had made so much progress in finding ways not to stand out, and now I was once again going to be the center of jokes and attention. Unable to sleep, I rose before dawn and made my way to Sergei's house.

It was still dark when I got there and there was no movement in the house. I climbed the fence to the back and knocked on the glass. He came to the window rubbing his eyes, his hair in a tousle.

"Get dressed," I said. "You're coming with me."

He met me in the street out front in rumpled clothes, his crutch tucked under his arm. I started leading him down the hill just as the sun was coming up. He looked at me, as if shaking himself out of a dream.

"Where are we going?"

"You don't want to miss any more school, do you?"

It took us an hour and a half to get to the school. Most of the students had already arrived. The morning air was cool and very still. We approached the steps of the school. My heart was beating hard, but I ignored it. I knew what I had to do.

A few people sitting at the bottom of the steps were the first to notice us. Then other heads started turning our way. A younger boy, probably a fourth- or fifth-grader, elbowed his friend in the ribs. There was no turning back. I slid my arm around Sergei's back. I lifted him up into my arms and started to carry him up the steps.

Everywhere people began to point. I kept climbing. Behind us someone let out a long pig-like squeal of laughter. I tried to keep my eyes focused just a few steps ahead of me.

The climb seemed like it would never end, as if I were scaling an escalator that was going backwards. I passed Benita, frozen with a look of astonishment. And from above, like two horrible predatory birds, Gloria and Marisol grinned down upon us.

They parted for us at the top without a word. I set Sergei down and together we walked to *Profesora* Ruiz's class to tell her that Sergei would be starting school again.

The rest of that day was full of whispered talk and laughter. I could feel people watching me, but I didn't look back. I told myself that as long as Sergei could keep smiling, I could bear it as well.

Every day for the rest of the school year, I met Sergei at the bottom of the hill before school and carried him to the top. And every day we endured jeers and taunts. I started getting into fights again, but *Profesora* Ruiz didn't try to punish me with extra assignments or make me stay after school. She did scold me privately after class, but the softness of her eyes told me she was on my side.

Sergei and I went back to our old schedule of late afternoons at his house. One day it occurred to me that there was no reason for him to always be confined to his house. I decided to take him the beach where Marisol and Gloria and I used to meet. So on the first day of summer, I carried him down the steep slope to the shore. It was there that he admitted to me that he that had started the rumors about us. He had been downtown and had seen Raúl Diego from our class and had told him everything about the time we had been spending together. I widened my eyes in pretend shock. I took his crutch and started to walk away as if to abandon him there for his crime.

"Margarita!" he called out. "Come back! Please! I'm sorry!"

I ran back to him, sweeping him up into my arms until we were both exhausted with laughter. He said my name over and over, his sandpapery Russian accent smoothing away the harshness of the consonants of a name I had always hated. We promised each other that as soon as our parents would allow it, we would marry, and we talked of how we would travel around the world attending his concerts and lectures. We would have a beautiful home that would always be full of music. And, when I was ready, he would even teach me to play. Every day the world around us shifted a little more, making room for new possibilities.

🌊 🌊 🌊

The letter from my father telling my mother to bring us to the United States came on the tenth day of summer. I was walking through the door, having just returned from taking Sergei to the Parque Teniente Guerrero, when my mother's glowing face told me everything I needed to know. We were to leave at once, she said, bringing only the clothes we needed. Papá would come back to Tijuana with one of my cousins to take care of selling our things and transferring ownership of the house to my mother's sister.

"Margarita is right," he wrote. "There is no reason for us to be apart any longer."

I had only enough time to see Sergei twice before we left. As I climbed the hill to his house, I felt a dull throbbing in my head. I went in without knocking and found him at the piano, running his fingers up and down the keys, releasing a spirited string of notes. I stood watching him for a long time, not knowing how to interrupt him, or what I would say. When he finally noticed me, he jumped up with his crutch and hobbled over to greet me, smiling as always.

It took me a long time to force the words out. I told him I would come back with my father in a few weeks to see him. I would be able to come back many times each year, especially if our new business did as well as my father was hoping. I said we would hardly have a chance to miss each other.

Sergei had little to say, but kept his smile up throughout. After all, he said, his concerts would someday bring him to the United States. In the meantime, we would write every day and keep in touch. There was no reason why we shouldn't someday fulfill our plans.

He turned back to the piano as I said goodbye. Leaving the house, I heard the same tune he had been playing when I had walked in. But now the notes were much slower, and further down the scale. It wasn't the same song at all.

That night, as my mother and I began to pack, I searched my belongings for something to give Sergei, something he could carry with him to remind him of me until I came back. But I could find nothing that was valuable to me, nothing that I thought would interest him.

In the closet I shared with my sister I found a container of red nail polish that I had once bought without my mother's permission and hidden in a shoebox. I took it with me the next morning when I went to see Sergei for the last time. With it, I painted my initials on his cast.

"You should just be getting this off by the time I come back," I said with a cheerfulness I had learned from him.

"I wish I had something for you," he said, and for the first time I could see the sadness seeping into his face like blue ink spreading through water.

I told him that it didn't matter. I told him I had everything I needed to remember him.

🙟 🙟 🙟

During my first week in Sacramento I wrote Sergei daily, sometimes even twice a day, telling him all the details of my new life. My father promised me that in time I would start to forget him, that the pain would become bearable. In the meantime, he said, it would help if I focussed on making new friends and adjusting to my new surroundings. Here, he told me, was a chance for me to make a fresh start with my life, just as he and Mamá were doing with theirs.

I got to work at once helping with the new business, boxing and loading the tamales that my uncle's wife made onto a truck behind his huge, gleaming kitchen. At night *Tío* Ramón gave me English lessons, which I picked up quickly. By the time summer was nearly over, I was speaking well enough to get by and had even made friends with a couple of girls who would be in my same class.

Over the next few months, life in Sacramento turned out not to be as wonderful as my father had said it would be, nor as bleak as Benita had foretold. It has now been four years since I last saw Sergei. Getting along with people here is no easier or more difficult than it was in Tijuana. The business has kept us all too busy to return to Tijuana as I had hoped we would. It will probably be a long time before I see the ocean again, but there is a river here. I like to go there on weekends, though sometimes this means going there by myself.

As my father predicted, I began little by little to forget Sergei. Today I can honestly say that I no longer miss him. But that does not mean that he is no longer with me, or that our story has come to an end. For because of him, every day I am left with the feeling that I am falling through my life rather than living it. I am falling, not the way that Sergei once fell, but the way I had once been told that the earth in its orbit is forever falling towards the sun, falling into it and soaring above it at the same time, always soaring and falling, falling and soaring.

RESTORATION

THIRTY MILES BEFORE THE MOUTH of the stretch of Highway 5 called the Grapevine, Chava launches into the *rancheras* he knows Ricky hates. He whistles hard and shrill above the rumble of the Impala's engine, giving it all the angry wind he's got.

Next to him his brother winces, tightens his white-knuckled grip on the wheel. "Could you it hold down, *hombre*," he says. "This heat. The dust. My head."

"Awww, poor baaaaaby." Chava reaches over and lifts up Ricky's sunglasses, revealing blood-shot eyes, deep bags beneath them. "Man, you look like a piece of shit. A giant piece of *cagada* with bad hair that's been lying out in the sun too long. No wonder Traci dumped you. Nobody wants to marry a piece of shit."

Ricky stays hunched and motionless. He's been up all night with a pint of Cuervo and he hasn't shaved and he's starting to smell. He keeps his eyes locked on the road, as if moving them even slightly right or left would cause searing pain.

"She'll come back," he mutters.

"Shuuuuure," Chava says. "And you know what? Tomorrow, donkeys are going to fly out of my ass doing the can-can. She's better off without you. Man, after what you did to her. . ."

He looks away, shakes his head. Heading up the block yesterday to his brother's apartment, he saw Traci hurrying down the front steps, red-faced and grousing to herself in Spanish. He figured they'd been fighting, or that Ricky had just stood her up again, so he snuck up behind her with the best dirty joke he knew to cheer her up. He caught her by the waist and spun her towards him. That's when he saw the bruise hovering below her eye, a red and blue oval, like a pinched rose petal.

"It isn't any of your business," Ricky says.

"Excuse me if I make it my business."

"You know how she exaggerates everything."

"Her face didn't exaggerate."

"It was the *first time*."

"There's *always* a first time," Chava says. "My job is to make sure it's the last. Now shut up and drive and don't fuck up my transmission."

He crosses his arms so that his biceps bulge enormously over his fists. He closes his eyes against the sun glaring off the hood and tries to think of something else, but a dull rage keeps at him, like a blunted icepick digging under his ribs. Chava dated Traci for a while before she and Ricky started going out five years ago, and in all that time yesterday was the first time he ever saw her cry. He's never known her to take shit from anybody—she's always known how to fling it back with twice the force. Even that time her place on Second was broken into while she was in bed, she'd pulled a .22 from her bedstand and shot the guy in the foot without so much as asking, "Who's there?" Then she'd held him there at gunpoint, gushing blood all over her shag carpet, until he was crying for her to call the cops. Chava can't help cracking a smile. He's always liked women who know how to take control, who put themselves first, who get on top without asking so they can do what they want to do in bed. Now that Chava thinks of it, Ricky's lucky Traci didn't pull a gun on *him*.

"I've just been to the cops," she told him last night when he went to check on her. "They're already looking for him. If I were you, I'd get him out of town. Get him the fuck away from me."

"Ricky can lay low from the cops for a while," Chava told her.

"How long can he lay low from my six brothers?" she said, jutting out her pointy chin and fixing him with diamond-hard eyes.

🙰 🙰 🙰

When Ricky starts looking like he's about to do a face-first into the steering column, Chava figures he's had enough for a while. He tells him to pull off at the next service area. Chava's already made him get up at four in the morning to pack, hasn't let him eat anything, and has made him do all five hours of driving. He figures he'll let him sleep for an hour before they finish the rest of the trip to L.A. Chava has a parts manager job set up for him there at Martínez's shop on Highland, where Chava used to work years ago before they moved up north. The easy in for the job is more than Ricky deserves, but maybe for a while it'll keep him out of the illegal shit he's been dealing recently. Last week, Ricky reported his GTO stolen off the Van Ness corridor, but he's really got it hidden away with Bernie the German until his insurance bonanza comes through. Then he'll strip the car down to nothing and sell the parts and split the profit with Bernie.

At the station, Ricky floats the car around to the pump, then Chava goes into the air-conditioned Mini-Mart. He brings a pint of orange juice and a tin of aspirin up to the counter. The cashier, a skinny wisp of a girl with freckles on her face and arms, backs off a little, flicks a glance at the surveillance camera. At 210 pounds of muscle, Chava looks like he could bend a crow bar just by looking at it. It's hard to find women that don't automatically assume he's a rapist or an ex-con. But when he gives her his sweetest smile, the blood flows back into her face, and she smiles back. He's learned how to put women at ease, to make them feel he's their protector, not a threat, and the next thing he knows, he's tucking the girl's phone number in his back pocket. Not that he'll have a chance to use it, but it never hurts, you never know.

Outside, Ricky has left the tank filling by itself and is stooped into the bubble-domed phone booth next to the men's room. Chava comes up from behind just as he's dialing. He reaches in front of him, crashes his fist down hard into the cradle of the pay phone.

"She doesn't want you bothering her," he says.

"You can't keep me from talking to her," Ricky says. "We can work things out. She still loves me."

Chava says nothing, keeps his fist locked in the cradle and glares down at him until Ricky skulks back to the car, swearing under his breath in Spanish.

Chava takes the quarter out of the change return and reinserts it. He promised to call Rosalie, the Salvadoran girl he took home from the Rockaway Club in Oakland where he hangs out when he has nothing to do, which these days seems like every night. They were supposed to get together last night and go out to Bay Meadows for the night races, something a little more romantic than the fast slam in the bed they started out with. It would have been the first real date he's had in months, but in the hassle of getting Ricky packed and out of town, he forgot all about calling her.

He gets her answering machine.

"Rosalie, it's Chava," he says after the beep. "I hope you're not too pissed. . ."

A clicking sound, then her voice slashes in. "It's *Rosemarie.* What happened with last night?"

"I'm sorry, *linda,* something came up with my asshole brother. I'll make it up to you. How about we try again on Wednesday?"

"I already told you, I work Wednesdays."

"What about Thursday?"

"I watch my sister's kids on Thursday."

"Friday. . ."

"Friday I'm washing my hair, Saturday I clean house, and Sunday I'm picking up my Nobel Peace prize. Sorry, baby, I think you missed your train. Have a nice life."

The dial tone hums in his ear.

He finds Ricky sleeping face up on the grass island under the Chevron sign. He drops the juice and aspirin on top of him, gives him a sharp kick in the ribs. Ricky bolts up, shielding his eyes.

"What the hell was that for?" he says.

Back in the car Chava takes over the driving, slips in a cassette of Tejano songs as they coast back onto the Interstate. The tape has some of the same *rancheras* on it that his father used to listen to: loud, tinny, emotional songs about fighting for women, about adoring women, about suffering in the name of women. When he was a kid, he used to go running from the room whenever his father played them. They were right up there on the Mexican culture scale with velvet bullfighter paintings and plastic castanets—the musical equivalent of a root canal. But somewhere he started listening to the words, and the words meant something to him. *In woman I put my faith and hope. Because of her my heart has been changed. I will belong to her until the day I die.* Somehow the words seeped into his beliefs, into that pool of things he wants to believe.

"When did you start listening to that crap?" Ricky says.

The rest and the aspirin have brought him back to life. He's sitting up and running a comb through his hair as he tries to get a whole view of himself in the vanity mirror.

"That's the same shit the old man used to torture us with."

"Shut up and listen to it," Chava says. "Listen to the words. You might learn something about how to treat women. Your problem is you never appreciate a good thing. Like that '64 Mustang we had. You never gave it the attention it deserved."

"I busted my ass working on that car."

"Then you went and sold it to Martínez for half of what it was worth. Man, that was the most beautiful thing we ever owned."

"I owed some people a lot of money," Ricky says. "You would have done the same thing."

"The point isn't the car, asshole. The point is respect."

"I thought you liked women to take care of themselves," Ricky says.

"Everybody needs some protecting."

Ricky blurts out a laugh. "Yeah, that's you. Guardian of the female race. What bullshit. You're the one who can't keep a woman for more than three weeks."

Chava adjusts his grip on the wheel.

"You're the one who can't keep your dick in your pants," Ricky says.

"Shut up," Chava says, glowering. "Unless you feel like walking over the Grapevine."

What Ricky's saying is true, but it's not like it sounds. Chava's not one of those manipulators who gets off on seeing how many women he can pack into a weekend. He doesn't go looking for women, they just seem to want to be close to him, to draw from his strength, to feel safe and protected by him. He's never known how to push them away, even the ones that aren't so good looking. He believes he can find something beautiful in every woman, if he just takes the time to look in the right places—their voices, their gestures, their laughter. Maybe that's his problem: he's too good at finding beauty.

"For the right girl," Chava says, "it would be different. If I had a girl like Traci. . ."

Ricky shoots him a scalding look. "Don't even think about it, you son-of-a-bitch."

"Think about what?"

"About anything that has to do with Traci. I'm not giving up on her." He leans back and lights a Pall Mall, releases a lazy swirl of smoke. "This is just a temporary setback. I know Traci. She needs time to calm down. In the meantime,"— he jabs at Chava with the cigarette—"keep your greasy hands off of her."

As the Grapevine starts to come into view, the temperature inside the car shoots up. Chava cranks down his window, but it doesn't help. After a few minutes Ricky takes a long pull on his cigarette and starts to laugh quietly.

"What's so funny, asshole?" Chava says.

"You don't think I know, do you?"

"Know what?"

"Oh," he says casually, "how you feel about Traci."

"I like Traci," Chava says. "I've always liked her."

"Sure you do, little brother," he says, grinning sideways at him. "I've seen the way you look at her, too. The way you straighten up when she comes into the room, the way you're all smiles for her, even if you're in a shitty mood. 'Can I get you a drink, Traci?' 'Can I straighten that fender for you, Traci?' 'Do you need a lift downtown, Traci?'"

Chava bites down on his words, focuses his attention on the license plate of a Mack he's stuck behind.

Ricky says, "You have this funny way of hiding your hands so she won't see the grease and paint. Did you know you do that? Hide your hands when she's around?"

Chava's jaw goes tense, vise-like.

Ricky laughs. "Hey, don't worry. I don't blame you. She's incredible, and you'd be an idiot if you didn't want her. I just want you to know I understand. I know why you're treating me like this. You never got over the fact that I took Traci away from you. Now you see a chance to get even, and. . ."

"That's bullshit," Chava says. "You didn't take Traci away from me, she . . ."

"That's right," Ricky says. "She dumped you. After—what? Two weeks? That's a record even for you. Face it. She was the best you ever had."

Chava loosens his grip on the wheel. He adjusts the vents towards himself, plucks at his sticky T-shirt. He knows better than to let Ricky get to him. Keep your eye on your goal, he tells himself. Just a couple more hours. Leave him at the motel, don't get out of the car, get the hell away from him.

After a few minutes Chava can't help thinking about Traci again. He has to admit, Ricky is right. Traci was different. She knew things that even the older women he had been with didn't. In bed she never let him cover her in a shelter of lovemaking. She didn't surrender to his size; she took control of it, made his strength her own, manipulating his body in ways that were exciting and frightening and humiliating. But more than this, she reached down into him and brought his heart out from its hiding place, brought it close to the surface, where he could feel it for the first time. *In my life you have been my delight, because you taught me how to love . . .*

Fuck you, Ricky, he thinks. Just fuck you.

In the distance, the San Bernadino Mountains bleed through the haze. Chava sinks his foot to the floor. Quiet rumbling fills the car.

"Look," Ricky says after a while. "I don't see why things have to be like this. Why don't we just try and get along?"

"Don't bullshit me, man," Chava says.

"This isn't bullshit. It's been bothering me for a long time. You're my brother, and I don't want us to always fight. Things used to be good between us. You remember."

"I remember bailing your bony ass out of jail on my birthday," Chava says. "I remember hiding you from the cops at the back of my shop. I remember fighting. That's what I remember."

"We did do a lot of fighting," Ricky says, grinning. "Remember this?"

He peals down his lower lip, exposing a moist glimmer of tooth, a gold canine. It flashes at Chava obscenely. The tooth is from the only time Chava ever hit Ricky, after he totaled Chava's '74 Camero by speeding the wrong way down a one-way. The punch to Ricky's face had chipped two teeth and knocked out a third. Now every time Ricky wants something, all he has to do is shine that tooth and Chava's stomach starts to buckle. Usually it works, and it's working now, but Chava turns his thoughts to the blur of mountains ahead.

"Come on," Ricky says. "Loosen up. Remember that time we drove out on 15 to the Mojave? We had a great time then, didn't we?"

"I don't remember that," Chava says.

"Of course you do. We were so drunk we couldn't see the road, but it didn't matter, because it was just us and a few coyotes and a lot of open space to do whatever the hell we wanted. We should do that again."

"You're not getting Traci back."

"Forget about Traci. This is about you and me. God damn you, we're brothers."

His voice has dropped to a raspy lilt, the way it does whenever he's trying to get out of something. Ricky can wet-sand over any conflict, making you forget what it was you were mad about. Maybe that's how he's kept it together with Traci for so long. Well, not anymore. Not if Chava has anything to say about it. Keep driving and stop listening, he thinks. Don't think. Drive.

✿⳾ ✿⳾ ✿⳾

When they get to the Grapevine, the road widens to five lanes as it begins its ascent through the scabbed mountains. The car's engine revs high, but keeps an even speed in spite of the altitude. It's a good car, a '61 Chevy SS he's been working on, though not nearly as powerful as the 'Stang he and Ricky used to own. That was the car that made him fall in love with repair work, a forest green First Series '64 and a half, the very first 'Stang model to come off the line. Together they spent thousands of hours searching junkyards for parts, bringing the car slowly back to sparkling condition before Ricky went and sold it behind his back to Juan Martínez in order to pay off a bunch of gambling debts.

Chava has always loved cars, especially American models from when he was a kid. But doing business with Ricky, he's found that nothing is what he thought it was. Everybody's ripping off somebody, nothing is totally clean, because if you play by the book, you'll never make the real money. Sure, Ricky's done him a favor showing him the reality of the business, but somehow he's also lost his love for cars. He wants that feeling back, the feeling of losing himself until sunrise in a garage with hammer and spoon until his ears ring, of watching an ugly, pocked-up heap just starting to get its pride back. That was just after he had met Traci, just before he had opened his own shop, long before he knew anything about getting around tax regulations. Life had seemed clear and open then, full of the possibilities that come with love, of things to believe in. But a couple of weeks later he made the same mistake he always made with women, only this time the mistake seemed to matter. He slept with another woman, a meter reader he had flirted with to avoid her giving him a ticket.

And then he had told Traci. He had only wanted to be honest. Calmly she told him not to call her again. He tried to plead with her, but she clamped her expression against him. Months later, she'd started seeing Ricky, which in a funny way Chava didn't mind at all, had even encouraged, because it brought Traci near him again. She was around the shop all the time now, and if he couldn't have her, he wanted her to be near. When he had proved to her that he wasn't jealous, they became friends again, careful with each other at first, then closer and closer as she began turning to him to try and better understand Ricky's mood shifts. All along Chava knew he was only waiting until Ricky's arguing and drinking drove her away. Chava would be there to catch her, her safety net, her shelter. But that never happened. Their fights always seemed to involve a bucking of foreheads, a kind of leaning together rather than a turning apart.

The smell of truck diesel seeps through the vents, making Chava slightly sick. The car levels off at the summit, then begins its descent, and soon Chava can see the smog blanket smothering the basin, all but deleting the edges of the skyline. He pops the tape out and fishes around the dial. In a few minutes a station announces a smog alert for the L.A area.

✿ ✿ ✿

Traffic is so jammed on the Hollywood freeway that it's nearly dark when they get to the motel. Chava's plan was to leave Ricky there, then drive all night back to Oakland, but the heat has sucked the life out of him, and his head is in a vise of pain from smog and allergies and lack of food. He doesn't think he can make it back without drifting off at the wheel. The motel is called the Blue Suede, a blue-and-pink shoebox wedged between a strip mall and a burrito shack on Santa Monica. It's just three blocks from Martínez Auto Body, where he and Ricky had their first jobs. At the desk he asks the fat manager for a double room. Staying the night, at least he can keep an eye on Ricky and keep him from harassing Traci for a few more hours. At the back side of the motel Chava helps Ricky get his stuff out of the trunk. They lug a couple of duffel bags up the outer stairs to a second floor room overlooking a pool shaped like a guitar.

"I'm glad you're staying," Ricky says. "This will give us a chance to set things straight. I don't want you leaving thinking I'm a complete asshole."

In the room, Chava kicks off his boots and lies back on the bed next to the night stand with the phone on it while Ricky starts unpacking. The breath of the air conditioner overhead feels good after the long, hot day. He closes his eyes for a moment, taking in the cool, flat air.

When the phone rings, inches from his head, Chava jolts out of sleep. He can hear the squeal of the shower head in the bathroom and Ricky singing a Rolling Stones song. Chava hates the Rolling Stones, hates all that kind of music. He rolls over, picks up on the third ring.

"Who is it?"

"Chava? It's Traci."

"Traci." He jolts upright, rigid, suddenly wide awake. "Traci, how are you?"

"I've been trying all afternoon. I thought you guys were supposed to check in around two."

"We just got here. Traffic. Accident on 5."

"The drive was okay otherwise?" Her voice is like cool water on his ear.

"Okay. Not bad."

"How's Ricky?"

"You don't have to worry about him," he says. "I have everything under control. How's that beautiful face recovering?"

The silence that follows is not like Traci. Chava feels the phone go slick in his palm.

"Look," she says. "Let me talk to him."

"To Ricky?"

"To the fucking Pope. Yes, Ricky."

"He's not here."

"You just said he was there."

"I meant here in L.A., not here in the motel."

"Look, have him call me, okay?"

"What do you want to talk to him for?"

She says nothing. He pictures her cheeks puffed in frustration, pictures her tossing her hair out of her face. "Just have him call me, okay?"

Her voice is suddenly soft and weepy, not the electric current of anger it was yesterday. It's a voice he knows—his own voice whenever he's done something stupid to a woman and is groping for a way to make it up to her.

"I don't know if he'll call you tonight," he says. "He's been talking about taking a couple of days to think."

"Just make sure he knows I called."

"Sure," he says. "Traci?"

"What?"

He runs his blackened finger nail over a crack in the surface of the nightstand. "Nothing. You take care of yourself, eh, Traci?"

He hangs up and starts punching his fist into the mattress as hard as he can, over and over, until it starts to ache, until his eyes are stinging with moisture.

When Ricky comes out of the bathroom, he is buttoning a long-sleeve white shirt with a shiny feather pattern on each front panel and fake pearl buttons. You'd never guess it was the same person stinking up his car earlier. He's shaved and he smells of pomade and his hair is combed back in an old-fashioned pompadour that crests high at the front in a slick black wave. He moves about like he's got springs for joints, practically dancing around the room as he puts on creased pants and good leather shoes and his belt and watch. The sight of him looking so good pushes Chava over the ridge into depression. He slumps back on the bed, drags a pillow over his face.

"Come on," Ricky says, kicking the bed frame. "Let's get some food. You haven't eaten since we left."

"How can you think about food?" Chava says.

After Chava has showered and changed into some of Ricky's clothes, which are tight and uncomfortable for him, they head next door to the burrito place that's all windows next to a service station. The place is cheap and clean, with a handwritten menu over the counter and wooden picnic tables painted black. Chava can tell the place is run by real Mexicans because there are jars of assorted whole chiles, the likes of which he hasn't seen since he was a kid, and there is a burnt scent of *mole* in the air. At the counter Chava reaches for his wallet, but Ricky flashes a twenty, says he'll pay. Chava gets a table while Ricky orders. He still hasn't told him about Traci calling, which is stupid because it's going to backfire on him. It's hopeless to try to keep them apart. Ricky always gets what he wants. Ricky always comes out smiling.

"Why so down?" Rick says, gliding a plate across the table to Chava. "Could it be that you're actually going to miss your big brother?"

Chava doesn't look at him. He digs into the burrito, which is saddled with a huge helping of beans. He thinks he has no appetite, but one mouthful triggers a surge of hunger. He reaches for the chile jar, fishes out a black one with a plastic spoon.

"I wouldn't eat the black ones," Ricky says.

Chava ignores him, pops one in his mouth. His tongue flares. He tries not to let on, but sweat starts seeping from his forehead, his scalp. He reaches for his beer, nearly tipping it over.

"You should listen to your big brother," Ricky says, shaking his head. "You never know. You might learn something."

❦ ❦ ❦

After they eat, Ricky wants to go out for beers, but Chava just wants to go back to the room.

"I'll pay," Ricky says. "I want to make things up to you. I want to prove to you that we can get along."

They drive east on Santa Monica to a place Chava remembers called Vega's, the noisiest place he can think of so that at least he and Ricky won't have to talk. The place is filling up with people in their early twenties, about half of them Mexicans, half Anglos. They take a booth on the raised platform that looks out over the bar and order from a waitress in loose jeans and heels. "I'll be with you in a minute," she says, and bumps Ricky with her hip. He smiles up at her, winks.

Chava notices a couple of young women in the booth across from them, watching them. They are leaning close to each other, talking and laughing as they stare. He and Ricky clearly stand out, because most of the locals are in T-shirts, whereas he and Ricky are looking a little too slick for this crowd.

"This was a good choice," Ricky says, leaning back. "I'm glad you're here. I know I've fucked up a lot lately. I want to make it up to you, clear the air."

Chava plunks his empty bottle down on the table. "Thanks for the beer and dinner. Consider us even on all counts."

"Come on, man. Why do you have to fight me on everything?"

"You're never going to change."

"I'm trying to change," he says. He digs his thumbnail under his beer label. "I'm even thinking about getting out of all this illegal crap."

"Sure you are. Now tell me about those plans to donate your money to the Church."

"Actually, I was thinking about taking up counseling troubled youth."

"Why not just go into the priesthood like Mom always wanted you to?" Chava says.

"You think that's funny? I happen to think I look quite good in black." He puts his palms together. "'Bless you, my child.'"

Chava tries to stifle a laugh, but can't. The waitress thumps down two more beers.

"There, you see?" Ricky says. "Aren't we getting along great?"

Chava takes a sip from the fresh bottle. He knows he's had enough, but the beer is making him feel looser, releasing the tension that has built up in his shoulders. When he looks over to the next booth, the two girls are still smiling at them.

"I think the one with the big chest wants you," Ricky says.

"Shut up and drink your beer," Chava says.

"I'm serious, *hombre*. And look at the legs on her friend."

Ricky raises his beer to them, and in a moment they are sliding out of their seats and making their way over.

"What the hell did you do that for?" Chava says.

"Maybe a little female company will help get the stick out of your ass."

"The two of you look like you're having fun," the shorter, big-chested one says. She's wearing a tight blue blouse and jeans, and the slant of her eyes gives her a devilish look.

"Carmen's radar is always up for where the best time is," the other one says. "If there's any fun to be had, you can bet she'll find it."

"Would you ladies care to grace our table with your company?" Ricky says, rising a bit.

"What do you think, Carmen? Do they look like gentlemen?"

"I'm willing to risk it," she says, and they slide into the booth on opposite sides. "I'm Carmen. This is Diana. And you two must be from out of town."

"How could you guess?" Ricky says, resting his chin on his knuckles.

"You look too friendly to be from L.A.," Carmen says.

"Actually, it's your clothes that gave you away," Diana says. Her voice, low and velvety, draws them towards her in order to hear.

"They're as smart as they are pretty," Ricky says to Chava.

"What do you boys do when you're not tearing up other people's towns?" Carmen says.

"I work when I feel like it," Chava says. "I run my own business."

"I told you," Diana says. "They looked like self-sufficient types. Didn't I tell you, Carmen?"

"Independence is good," Carmen says, "but everybody needs somebody to rely on."

Diana moves a little closer to Ricky, smiles at him. Ricky smiles back, lets his eyes run the course of her long, tight figure. Chava feels his stomach turn. He takes a sip of cold beer.

Into their next round of beers, Carmen starts talking about how much she hates her boss, who's always complaining to her about things that aren't her responsibility. Her voice is louder than Diana's and cuts easily through the bar noise. She goes on for several minutes at high idle. Diana adds nothing, inches a little closer to Ricky. She picks something out of his hair. Ricky smiles, gives her his best shy-little-boy act. He's never had a problem attracting women, but if he's ever fooled around on Traci, he's certainly never let on. Which is a good thing, because as Chava knows, that's the one thing that will push Traci over the edge. If she even suspects something like that. . .

Diana laces her fingers over Ricky's shoulder, whispers something in his ear. Chava leans back. He takes a long pull at his beer.

A few minutes later the girls get up to greet some friends they notice have just come in and are standing at the bar. "It's nice to have met some real gentlemen," Diana says.

"Don't go too far away," Carmen says.

Ricky and Chava watch them descend the steps to the bar. Each girl looks over her shoulder once and waves.

"Look," Chava says, turning to Ricky. "I want to be with the Talker. Why don't we split up. You take her friend. We'll meet at the motel in the morning."

"They're just having fun with us," Ricky says. "They're not serious."

"What are you talking about? It was your idea to talk to them. You invited them over."

"I was just messing around," Ricky says. "I was trying to get you to loosen up."

"Come on," Chava says. "You can't tell me you don't like her friend with the voice."

"I don't mess around. I've got Traci to think about."

"Don't give me that. You can't tell me that in five years . . ."

"I'm serious. I flirt, but I don't fuck around on Traci."

Chava stares at him, waiting for a crack in his expression to show he's lying. But there's nothing.

"Come on," he says. "She likes me. If you don't at least play nice with her friend, you're going to ruin my chances. We were getting along great. Why do you want to fuck everything up now?"

Ricky looks over at the bar. Diana's still watching. She raises her bottle to them. Then, eyes fixed on Ricky, she brings the bottle to her mouth, letting her lips linger suggestively around the stem.

"I don't know," he says.

"All you have to do is talk to her," Chava says in a low voice into Ricky's ear.

Ricky keeps looking.

"Nobody's going to know anything," Chava says. "Then, afterwards, we can go out to the desert like you wanted. Just the two of us."

"I don't know, man. It's just that Traci. . ."

"It's over with you and Traci."

"It's not over with me and Traci."

"All right. It's not. You'll get Traci back. But right now you're not with Traci. She ran you out of town. She ended it. You can do anything you want to, *hombre*. Technically speaking, anyway."

Chava is up so close to Ricky he can see a vein in his throat pulsing in double-time to the music. Chava hears him mutter, "technically."

"Don't fuck this up for me," he says. "You don't know how long it's been since I've gotten anything good."

Ricky keeps staring.

"Go ahead, brother," Chava says, in a voice so low, so subliminal, he almost can't hear his own words.

A few minutes later Ricky goes down to the lower bar. Chava watches him carefully, the way he stumbles through the crowd, tucking his shirt in at the sides. Diana greets him, puts a hand on his shoulder. They turn toward the bar so that Chava can't see their faces. But he can tell by the way Ricky's hands keep moving that they're talking. Soon Diana is laughing, leaning close to him again, speaking into his ear, letting her lips hover there. She begins gliding her hand up and down his back, in short little strokes at first, then more fluidly, sweeping all the way up and down, dropping a little lower each time until her fingers are brushing the back pockets of Ricky's pants. A beer sign over the bar flashes red, yellow, green, red . . .

Carmen comes back to the table soon, slides in next to Chava and squeezes his bicep with both hands. "You certainly are a big guy," she says. "I'll bet you spend a lot of time at a gym."

"Sure," Chava says. "You could say that."

"You're the serious one, aren't you? I can tell. There's always one brother that's the serious one."

"I guess so," he says.

"Aren't you having a good time?" she says.

"Sure. Sure I am," he says, but he's not really listening. Diana has her hand tucked in Ricky's back pocket now, but Ricky's still just standing there stiff as a jack post. Chava sees Ricky order two more beers. He gets his change back, then finally settles an arm around her waist. He slides his middle finger through her belt loop, pulls her closer.

"So," Chava says, turning to Carmen and looking her up and down as if for the first time. "Did you two pretty flowers come together?"

"Diana drove," she says. "I couldn't get my car started."

"Maybe I could take a look at it for you. That is, if you don't mind going back to your place."

She shakes her finger at him. "I thought you were a gentleman," she says.

"That's a lonely business," he says. "And overrated."

Below they meet up with Ricky and the other girl. They are leaning against each now. Their laughter is infectious, and soon all four of them are laughing at nothing in particular.

Outside of the bar Chava pulls Ricky aside. "I'm driving the Big Mouth home." He slips him the key to the motel room. "Get her out of there by sunrise, eh?"

As Chava and Carmen head to the car, he gets his first good look at her under the glare of the street light. She looks older that he thought she was, and he sees wrinkles where her breasts come together. Her make-up is thick enough that you have to wonder what she's hiding. She's not his type, really, a little stocky, but well put-together enough.

In the car she stretches her legs out and unstraps her shoes. She seems much drunker than she did in the bar, rolling her head from side to side as she talks, like a flower on a broken stem. She reaches into her purse for a cigarette.

"Sorry," Chava says. "No smoking in the car." He has no idea why he says this. He always lets people smoke in his car. She raises her eyebrows at him, drops the cigarettes back in her purse.

"It's a nice car," she says, patting the seats and looking around her.

"It's a '61. They only sold a hundred and forty-two of these. They're pretty rare."

"Oh," she says. He takes her hand and smiles at her, searching for that thing about her that is most attractive, the thing he can focus on. She moves a little closer, and he leans to kiss her. But her lips are slack and wet, like she's been kissed too many times. Like rotted fruit, he can't help thinking. He turns the ignition on and pulls away from the curb.

By the time he finds the freeway, she is into a story about how she was ripped off sixty dollars at the swap meet last weekend. Chava lets her voice wash over him, focuses on his driving so he won't get pulled over. By the time they reach her building, she has been talking non-stop for twenty minutes.

He comes around to her side of the car to let her out. "It was great to meet you," he says. "L.A. is lucky to have such beautiful women. You really made my evening."

"There's no reason it has to end now, is there?"

"I'm pretty tired," he says. "I've been driving all day, and I want to leave early tomorrow to beat the heat."

"Don't you want to come in and see my place?"

"I'm sure it's beautiful," he says. "But I've got to drive back in the morning."

"Oh, just come in for a drink," she says. "Five minutes."

"Call me if you're ever up north," he says, but makes no move to give her his number, and she makes no move to leave. Her face tenses, lines appearing where none had been before. Suddenly she doesn't seem drunk anymore.

"I just wanted to make sure you got home safe," Chava says.

She slams the door, striking the roof once with her purse as she turns away. Chava winces. She heads up the pathway. Chava watches her until she disappears beyond some high hedges, waiting for anything about her to jump out at him. When she is out of sight, he leans his forehead against the car roof. He runs his fingertips gently over the surface of the paint.

ఌ ఌ ఌ

Chava thinks about driving around the city all night, but he's still drunk and doesn't want to get pulled over. Instead he drives back to the motel, stopping for all yellow lights and staying in the right lane. He doesn't see any sign of Diana's car when he gets to the motel, but he doesn't want to risk going up to the room yet. The blue reflection of the pool is casting serene waves against the side of the building. He hops the locked gate to the pool area and hunkers down at the water's edge. Tomorrow he will call Traci and tell her everything. Not just about Ricky, but about what he, Chava, still feels for her, has always felt for her. He'll tell her all the things he has already told her in his dreams, and other things, too. That he was a fool to hurt her, to let her push him away. That he has to come back to her, wants to protect her with the strength of his body and be protected by the strength of her spirit. Take me back, he will say. Traci, I love you. *Because you won't love me I turned to vice, I'm rolling in sin. Love me and bring me back to the world of the living,* Traci, Traci . . .

Soon he is crying, tears flowing down his face with an urgency that seems to have little to do with his own thoughts. And he realizes that he is not crying just for Traci, but for everything in his own life that has somehow gotten twisted out of his grasp.

After a long while he stretches out on one of the lounge chairs, face up under the stars. Yes, he can actually see stars, about a dozen of them, in spite of the smog and city lights. The air is warm and still. And even the traffic on Santa Monica is like a voice hushing him.

🙬 🙬 🙬

When he wakes up, the sun is just bending over the motel roof. He goes up the steps to the room, turns the knob carefully. The door opens.

Ricky is not in his bed, or in the bathroom. Chava goes to the window, draws back the curtain. There's no sign of Ricky.

With Ricky gone, now is the time to call Traci. But when he picks up the phone, he finds that his resolve from last night is gone. He tries to recall all the things he wanted to say to her, but the words aren't there anymore. Yes, he must have been pretty drunk last night. He sets the receiver down and leans back against the headboard.

Still, he thinks, there is no reason he should not tell her about Ricky. If Chava can't have her, then Ricky, who deserves her even less, isn't going to have her either. At least Chava isn't going to make it easy for him.

Dialing the number isn't as easy as he thought it would be. He tries to think of how he should sound when he tells her, what words he will use. But a hangover is keeping him from thinking. His vision pulses. Don't think about Ricky. Dial. Tell her.

Just as he is pressing the receiver to his ear, there is rattling at the door, and Ricky comes in, noisily whistling one of the same *rancheras* they had been listening to in the car. His arms are loaded with grocery bags, his hair tied back in a blue bandana. The smile on his face reminds Chava of what he used to look like when they were teenagers.

He drops the bags on the counter and starts unloading them—a six-pack of Coors, a Monster Size bag of Doritos, a French loaf, a block of cheddar the size of a wheel block, pretzels, two butcher-wrapped deli sandwiches, two more six packs. . . .

"Where have you been?" Chava says.

"Out," he says. "Thinking about Traci. I need to get my shit together if I'm going to make things work with her. You made me realize that."

"How was Diana?"

"I didn't do anything. I told you last night, I couldn't do that to Traci."

"Don't bullshit me. I know you . . ."

"You don't know me," Ricky says, turning towards him suddenly. "You're always so fucking ready to judge, but you don't know me." He goes back to unloading the groceries.

Chava watches his back for a few minutes. "What's all that shit?"

Out of his back pocket Ricky takes a Triple A map, unfurls it with a flick of his wrist. The blue and red veined state of California spreads down to his toe. "We're going to the desert," he says. "I've got enough food to last us two days—well, enough beer, anyway."

"I have to be at the shop," Chava says. "I don't have time for this."

"I've got something I bet will change your mind." He tosses the map on the bed and heads out the door.

A few seconds later Chava gets up and follows. Passing the Coke machine on the second floor, he sees it in the lot below, parked at an angle so that it takes up two spaces: a gleaming, forest green '64 Mustang. In the brilliant sun, the chrome hubs shine. Going down the steps, he notices that they look like originals.

"Where did you get that?"

"I'm watching it for Martínez. Recognize it?"

"Of course. '64 and a half. First Series. Like the one we used to have."

"Look closer," Ricky says.

Chava takes a few steps down, then stops.

"That's right," Ricky says. "It *is* our car. Martínez never got rid of it. It's his favorite, likes to enter it in car shows. I went to talk to him about that job and told him I'd get him some free Buick parts I know about if he'd lend it to me for a couple of days."

Down below, Chava gets closer and looks the car over. He can't help staring at the expert exterior work—no sign of dings or dimples or amateur blending, no matter how he angles his vision against the surface. He follows the striping down the door, steps around to the back, touches the dual exhaust tips. He and Ricky had never managed to get the chrome to look that good. Chava wipes his brow. Heat waves are already surging up obscenely from the pavement around him, but the cool green exterior glints invitingly.

He walks all the way around the car, his eyes never leaving its surface. When he is back to the point where he started, he says, "Has he put a lot of miles on it?"

"Not many. It's mostly for show."

"Reproduction hubs?"

"Originals."

"Under the hood?"

"Like it just came off the line."

Chava gets closer to the driver's side, leans his head in through the open window into the taupe interior. He glances at the dials, the original radio. The bucket seats are replacements, but good ones, with blind pleats, hand-sewn. In the back he notices that the end caps have come together unevenly, but for the most part, it's an incredible job, better than his own upholsterer could have done.

"It's beautiful," Chava says. "Take it out and have fun with it. I'm heading back north."

"Just one day," Ricky says.

"The shop's waiting for me."

"You can do the driving. Don't you want to try her out?"

Chava starts heading back to the room, but Ricky grabs his sleeve. "It'll be like the old days," he says. "Like that time we headed out to Vegas to blow that money the old man gave us for graduation."

"We never did that," Chava says.

"You don't remember? We took 15 out through the Mojave and then broke down and had to wait six hours for another car to come by?"

"I don't remember ever going to Vegas."

"We never made it to Vegas. We spent all our money at the service station. We only had enough left for a tank of gas and a couple of six-packs."

"I don't remember."

Chava tries to turn back towards the motel, but it's not Ricky's grip on his sleeve that is preventing him. Chava does remember. Not clearly. Not distinctly. But for the first time in a long time he allows himself to remember. Something about an argument with a mechanic trying to overcharge them for a fan belt. A six-pack exploding from heat in the back seat. The memory edges its way into his mind like a knife prying at the edges of a gasket. More images flicker through. A joyride that took them to the border of the regional park. Drinking and smoking pot and shouting against the vast, arid silence at 3 AM, then getting caught in a rainstorm that came and went in five minutes. The clearing sky. And then stars—thousands upon thousands of them shining in a clear, pure, shimmering expanse of sky.

Closing his eyes against the heat, against the smog, Chava surrenders to the memory. If he tries, he thinks he might even be able to believe again. Believe in . . . believe in . . . what? Believe in . . . just . . . believe.

When Chava opens his eyes, Ricky is holding the car keys out to him, dangling them between thumb and forefinger. Under the noonday sun they sparkle, as if with some kind of promise, false or true: the promise of return, of restoration.

WHO IN THE MODERN WORLD CAN KEEP UP WITH JULIA JUÁREZ?

JULIA JUÁREZ LEAPT THROUGH THE SHOWER CURTAINS and slid three feet across the wet porcelain tiles. She grabbed the towel rack with one hand for balance. She shoved open the window, letting the breeze suck the steam from the room. She had overslept for the party the girls were throwing for her at Marta's Silver Palm Cantina. Once again those *pachucos* in 203 had kept her up and wide-eyed past two, blaring Chichi Méndez albums through her ceiling.

The telephone started ringing for the second time that morning. She rushed to the bedroom with a towel clasped around her bosom, a tube of toothpaste in her fist. She dashed the wet hair out of her eyes. She snatched up the receiver.

Once again she caught only the click of someone hanging up—probably Vida Benevides checking to see if she was on her way. This afternoon's get-together was supposed to be a surprise to celebrate her appearance on Friday's Local Hero's segment on the Channel 14 news. But yesterday her friend Connie had swept into her office on her lunch hour, recklessly waving a cig-arette as she sputtered all the details. She couldn't risk Julia showing up late, she'd explained, since some of the women were driving all the way up the Peninsula to be there. Besides, it wasn't every day one of your friends single-handedly stopped a criminal in his tracks—or for that matter, ended up rubbing elbows with a good-looking reporter like Andy Ramírez.

Julia slipped into her favorite outfit, a red and gray knee-length herring pattern off the discount racks in South City and, instead of a blazer, a bright red wool cape that her friend Vida had altered to look like this month's num-ber in the I. Magnin window. It was the same suit she had worn the week before when she had tracked Michael Alzamora, the head of a big bookkeep-ing firm downtown, to the Sunset Room of the Palace Hotel. She had learned by eavesdropping on two secretaries in a coffee shop that Alzamora was look-ing for a new office assistant, a perfect fit for her friend Ime. Julia had spun by his office that day and chummied up to the receptionist to find out where he was having lunch. At the hotel, she'd strolled past the maitre d' and the brilliant buffet tables and dropped her purse into the chair next to him. "I've got a friend who's a regular genius with numbers," she'd begun, playing up her Spanish accent in case he didn't recognize her as a fellow Chicano.

She smiled to herself as she remembered the crazy adrenaline rush. This had been the cornerstone of her life's successes: to live by a combination of instinct and a little practice, like a salsa step you improvise, or a Canasta play you make without thinking.

She yanked a bright red pump onto each foot, staggered once, did a few steps to the music coming from the neighbor's apartment. She tugged her belt to a fresh notch. She pinned her hat at a daring slant.

◆○◆ ◆○◆ ◆○◆

On the 48 bus she held on at the front and looked over the other passengers. Her car had been in the shop for three days, and she now found herself riding the same clunky, rust-colored buses that as a girl she had dreaded taking with her family to discount food stores and flea markets. Towards the back, a group of glared at her as they sat running combs through their hair—the same gang member-types with obscene words tattooed across their knuckles that had terrorized her when she was in high school. Her father had promised to move the family to a safer neighborhood, away from the grimy, violence-tinged streets of the Mission. But even with two jobs he hadn't been able to keep up with rent increases. Even now her heart ached at the memory of his face as he told her and her three sisters that they would have to move into an apartment even smaller than the tiny two-bedroom they had grown up in. At eighteen Julia had sworn she would move out of that neighborhood for good, would never ride another bus or have a meal out of a dented can.

But Julia had never been able to leave the Mission completely, had never moved more than a half-mile away, in spite of the fact that her job as a real estate agent had opened up the entire city to her. Most of her friends still lived there and had come to rely on her to seek out bargains and inexpensive rental units and even decent paying jobs. She checked classifieds weekly for her friends, intruded on conversations in elevators, dropped in on Mexican secretaries downtown for leads. In helping her friends, Julia had found a taste of a kind of justice that her father had told her never to expect. Every success on behalf of her friends, as well as every success of her own, went towards evening up the score of an unfair past.

At 24th and Mission, she was the first one off and into the street.

At once she saw Vida Benevides coming up the Bart station escalator. Julia placed two fingers between her teeth and gave a whistle, then waved. At the top of the escalator Vida made a complete turn to show off her outfit, a crisp, solid navy two-piece that clung to her petite hourglass figure.

Julia weaved through stalled traffic, rapping on hoods of cars with one hand, waving with the other. "Please," she called out, "you don't have to make a display."

"I got all of my bad habits from you," Vida yelled, shaking her pocketbook at her. "I'm tiny, but I make sure people see me coming."

They hugged lightly and began walking quickly together side by side. They talked over pedestrians and over each other, breaking apart to pass people, and coming together again still in conversation.

"I went to see Pilar Chávez again," Vida said. "The first thing she said when I walked in was, 'I see riches and beauty in store for you.' What a nerve. I said, 'I'm already beautiful, you ridiculous woman. I'm not opening my pocketbook until you tell me something new.'"

"*Ay*, Vida, don't tell me you actually believe that nonsense."

"Please," Vida said. "What do you take me for? Pilar knows all the people who own properties around the park. For twenty bucks she gets me leads on anybody looking to sell. That duplex on Dolores you've been eyeing? The owner's four months behind on her payments and doesn't speak a word of English. I'm sure she'd love to have a sympathetic Mexican represent her before she goes under."

"Vida, you amaze me."

She linked arms with Julia and beamed a smile up at her. "I know it," she said. "When have I ever let you down?"

At 22nd and Mission they cut right, past the Tower Theatre and east of the towering palms. It was the same route they used to take on their way home from high school together nearly a decade ago. They had become friends after some *chola* girls had started harassing Vida on the school's front steps, knocking her books from her hands and kicking her as she tried to pick them up. Julia had later found her crying behind the gymnasium. She had felt all the anger of her life pour out of her. "What the hell are you crying for?" she'd yelled. "You're giving them exactly what they want." Julia had made her follow her around for the rest of the day, lecturing her about how not to be taken advantage of. From then on, they found that as long as they stuck together, they were never harassed with anything more than words.

They crossed the street to avoid the mist from men spraying down the sidewalk in front of the produce markets. At 22nd and Capp, Vida said, "There's something I have to tell you about this afternoon, Julia. I shouldn't, but I know how much you hate surprises."

"I already know about the party," she laughed. "I promise not to let on."

"There's something else, though." She slipped on a pair of oversized sunglasses, as if to protect herself from Julia's reaction. "Nina Gutiérrez is going to be there."

Julia stopped. "You're joking. You know I'm not talking to her."

"I swear it wasn't me. Connie and I ran into her downtown. Connie remembered you knew her. She started talking, and, well, the next thing I knew . . ."

"Couldn't you have stopped her?"

"What was I supposed to do? Kick her in the shins to shut her up? But you are in a mood today. What do you think of my outfit? *¿Muy suave, no?* You'll have to try it on, but of course, I have a smaller waist than you, don't take offense."

"How many times have I told you to consult with me before you buy anything?" Julia said. "I know where you could have gotten it for half of what you paid. And that scarf. Really, Vida. What kind of state were you in when you went shopping for that?"

❧ ❧ ❧

When they got to Marta's, Julia had Vida go in ahead of her. Outside, she paced, fingering the clasp of her cape. She had recently had a falling out with Nina after the sad, broad-faced woman had told Julia that she wouldn't be needing her anymore to baby-sit her daughter Monica. Julia had been keeping an eye on the nine-year-old a couple times a month ever since the family had moved into the Ventana complex. But now, Nina said, Monica had stopped doing her homework and had even called her father a *pendejo*. As if this were Julia's fault. As if she were some kind of evil influence. But she warned herself that now was not the time to make an issue of it. She summoned up as natural a smile as she could. She pushed her way through the glass door.

The women at the back table, the only people in the bar, greeted her with a burst of applause and whistles. They had strung yellow streamers from the brass lamps over the bar and had outlined the door frames with white paper flowers. Julia pressed a palm to her bosom in mock surprise. "Stop," she said. "You guys will use any excuse to have a few beers on a weekday."

"Look at her," Connie boomed. "She loves the attention."

Beer in one hand, she minced over in heels and glitter stretch pants and pinched Julia's cheek as she kissed her. The other women crowded around too, buzzing with congratulations. Marta, the squat, frowning woman who owned the bar, gestured for the bartender to turn up the music. A Tina Ruiz number that was popular in the clubs sent Connie into an unsteady shimmy.

Nina waved girlishly at her from the edge of the group. She was in a cool, powder-green dress that sagged loosely under the arms. Julia took her hand so she would know there were no hard feelings. Marta swirled her apron in the air to get everyone seated. She licked her thumb and started firing cards around the table for canasta.

"Let's hear the real story," she said. "I don't trust anything those bastards say on TV."

Julia scraped her chair close and started to tell about how she and Vida had been rounding the corner into the parking lot across from Mission Quick Cleaners when they spotted a half-dozen kids in dark shirts crouched around the driver's side of her car. They started to scatter in all directions, except for one kid with a crow bar in one hand and a wire hanger in the other. He froze with his back to the car just long enough for Julia to ask him what in the world he thought he was doing. When he started running, Julia dropped her groceries and slipped behind the wheel. She swung out onto Capp, breaking left in time to see him disappear down Lilac. She cut left onto Mission, ran a light, then left again against traffic and up onto the sidewalk, cutting him off on 25th with a screech of rubber. He tumbled forward onto the hood, then flew back down the alley the way he had come, to where two cops Vida had pulled out of a Mission Street *taquería* were waiting.

"The next day Channel 14 called and said they wanted to send someone out to talk to me."

Connie released a squeal of delight. "Our very own TV personality."

"You guys are going to get yourselves killed one of these days," Marta rasped.

"*¡Fregona!* Watch what you say about my friend!" Vida put her arm around Julia. "Haven't you learned by now? Nobody messes with Super Chicana."

Laughter swept around the table. The bartender began setting down a round of beers. Across from Julia, Nina sat twirling a pendant string around her finger, so tightly that her finger had turned pearly white. "Weren't you frightened?" she said. "What if he had tried to hurt you?"

"They were just a bunch of punk of kids," Vida said dismissively.

"Anyway, you have to take things into your own hands sometimes," Julia said.

"I just hate to see people so desperate," Nina said. "I don't understand what's becoming of the Mexican people."

"And what do we look like?" Julia said. "Japanese tourists?"

"I don't mean that," Nina said. "But look at everything we've had to give up just to get where we are?"

"Like what?" Vida said. "Refried beans? My heart is breaking."

Nina shook her head sadly. "I guess sometimes it just comes down to making choices."

"Who's holding the game up?" Marta said, then lit a cigarette and blew smoke out of the corner of her mouth.

Nina sorted her cards, squinted at them through the smoke. Carefully, she layed down the first canasta.

When she got up to use the restroom a few minutes later, Vida said, "So who invited The Personality?"

"She seems so sad," Connie said, her mascara accenting her worried eyes. "I feel sorry for her."

"Don't be conned," Marta said. "She's trying to distract us so she can clean up, and it's working."

She started to peel Nina's cards off the table, but Vida stopped her with a chop to the wrist.

When Nina came back, Julia said, "So tell us, Nina. What would you do to save the Mexican people?"

"Oh, I wouldn't presume to have answers," she laughed.

Vida shrugged, flicked a card. "We can't be expected to carry the whole race with us."

"Mexicans don't want other people helping them, anyway," Connie said. "Especially the men. A bunch of machos."

"They want to keep women weak," Vida said.

"In order to hide how worthless they are in comparison," Julia said.

"I don't know about that," Nina said. "I know plenty of decent men."

"Traditional types." Julia rolled her eyes dismissively. "Nostalgic crooners."

"Anyway," Vida said, "it's not like none of us ever gave anything back."

"That's right," Connie said. "Look at everything Julia does for people."

"Even so, sometimes it seems . . ." Nina's face deepened. "Oh never mind," she laughed, " I'm slowing the game down. It's my turn, isn't it?"

"What?" Julia said. "Please tell me."

"Well," she said, "it's just that sometimes the way you talk . . . well, you sound almost as if . . . you hate your own people."

"Believe me," Julia said, "I know I'm made out of beans and tortillas just like everybody else. But sometimes you have to pretend you're better than everyone just to convince yourself that you're even half as good."

"Not everyone can keep up with you," Nina said.

"You would deny your daughter the chance to try?" Julia said.

No one said anything for a few minutes. Then a breeze from across the room drew everyone's attention to the far side of the bar.

A stocky, plum-dark Mexican girl was watching them from the open doorway, the bright sky behind her outlining broad hips and stout legs in a wide stance. She held the door open with a cocked foot. A stir of air shifted the black hair about her shoulders.

She came forward, letting the door suck shut behind her. She stopped in the middle of the room with all her weight on one foot, hip thrust out, fists sunk deep in the pockets of an oversized bomber jacket. Her jaw silently worked a piece of gum as she looked them over.

"We're not open," Marta said. "You'll have to come back later."

The girl rubbed her nose, then pointed the tip of her jacket wing at Julia. "I want to talk to the lady in red," she said.

Julia squinted at her against the bright afternoon light. "Who are you?" she said. "What do you want?"

"I'm Dotty Martínez. I recognized you on the bus this morning from the TV news. My brother was one of the kids who tried to break into your car. I wanted to pay you for the damage. I'm not working, but I have a little money saved."

Julia looked her up and down. Cuffless black chinos, worn to a charcoal color at the knees, sagged over china-doll shoes. Glossy, burgundy lipstick gave her a bruised, pouting look.

Julia waved her hand. "Forget it," she said. "It's just a couple hundred bucks. It's not worth the trouble." She tried to turn back to her cards, but Dotty came closer.

"I thought you might be able to do something for my brother," she said. "He's not a bad kid. I thought maybe if you talked to the juvenile authorities . . ."

Julia laughed. "You have some nerve," she said. "Anyway, it's out of my hands. But I wouldn't worry. I'm sure he'll just get a slap on the wrist."

The girl dropped her gaze. She blushed fiercely. "It's not the first time he's been caught." she said. "There was another time. They're not going to be so lenient."

"Why should Julia help you?" Vida said.

"My brother was supposed to enroll at the Art Institute next month. He wants to learn mechanical drawing, to work on automotive books, and he's got a lot of talent. But now he might not get to. I'm not trying to make excuses for him, but this is his one chance to really do something. I already have one brother in jail and I don't want . . ."

Her breathing became shallow as she talked. She reached for a chair to steady herself, took a white metal canister from her pocket and pressed it to her lips. Her body heaved gently as she inhaled. Then the canister disappeared back into her pocket.

"Look," she said after a moment, "I'm not used to asking for favors. Please think about it, lady. We'll do whatever you ask." She placed a crumpled piece of paper with her number on it in front of Julia. She turned and was out the door.

No one said anything for several seconds. Over the radio a woman's excessively happy voice was, in Spanish, pitching Tide detergent.

"Now I've seen everything," Vida said.

"What do you suppose was wrong with her?" Connie said, wide-eyed.

"Nothing that a kick in the ass wouldn't fix," Vida said.

"What are you going to do, Julia?"

"I don't see what I can do," Julia said. "Even if I wanted to."

Connie picked up her cards. "I guess it wouldn't be right to interfere with justice," she sighed. The women went back to their game. But as they played, Julia could feel Nina's eyes on her—dark, sad, questioning eyes that seemed saturated with all the worry of the world.

"Who's holding the game up?" Marta grumbled.

"Didn't that girl's story affect you?" Connie said.

"Not as much as losing is going to affect my wallet," she said. "I didn't say that. The devil made me say that."

"The devil makes you say a lot of things," Vida said.

"I know it," she sighed, laying down her winning cards. "We're pretty good friends."

✿ ✿ ✿

Julia saw Vida to her train, then turned down Mission to look into store windows while she waited for the next bus. She stepped around two men arguing drunkenly in front of a tobacco shop. She stopped and looked into the Great Value store, watched the women sorting through bins of tangled clothes for bargains for their kids, just as her own mother had once done for her. It was ridiculous to think that she could possibly hate her own people. But, at the same time, did she really care as much as she thought she did? In wanting justice, something had gone out of her, leaving her feeling as vacant as the properties through which she toured her clients. A sense of panic rose in her as she saw herself for the first time as Nina must have: a pushy woman in a red suit. A woman with great influence over trivial things.

On the bus home, she let this image of herself sharpen in her mind. She didn't turn away from it. Sometimes it took an outside push, even from someone as unlikely as Nina Gutiérrez, to redirect you towards the next phase of your life.

At home that evening after dinner Julia settled into a low chair in her living room. She searched her purse for the Ruiz girl's number, then steadied the phone in her lap. As carefully as if her soul depended on it, she pressed out the pattern of seven numbers.

✿ ✿ ✿

They arranged to meet the next morning at the coffee shop near the Victoria theatre. Julia drove by the station first for Vida in the red Impala she had borrowed from Martha. She had to let Vida in on the driver's side. An accident Marta had been in had left the passenger door jammed.

"I don't know why I agreed to this," Vida said as she slid across the seat. "If we leave now, we can still catch the half-day sale at Emporium."

"Just stick with me," Julia said. "I have a really good feeling about this."

On 16 she swung into a bus stop and turned the car over to Vida.

In the coffee shop it took Julia a couple of minutes to adjust to the dimness. She found Dotty towards the back, hugging her knee to her chin. She looked more mature than before, her hair pulled back with a clasp. She straightened up as Julia sat down across from her.

Before Julia could say anything, Dotty jumped into the same explanations she had given at Marta's. She spoke in a rushed whisper, leaning forward with hands splayed, fingertips pressed white against the tiled table top.

When she had finished, Julia said, "I intend to go to the police and talk to them. The one I had the most contact with was Méndez, or Menéndez. We seemed to get along pretty well. I can't promise anything, but he's a Chicano, and maybe I can. . ."

She took Julia's wrist in both hands. "Thank you, *señora*. I knew you would help me. I can't tell you how much . . ."

Julia raised her hand. "Let me finish. There's something else."

"I told you, lady, I'll pay for your car. I have a hundred in the bank . . ."

"I want you to let me help you."

Dotty's eyelids fluttered. She stopped chewing her gum.

"There's a lot I can do for you," Julia said. "You said you weren't work-ing. I think I can find you something. Nothing fancy, just some filing, that sort of thing to start. You wouldn't have to exert yourself. Later on, I could see what else I could arrange for you. You'll have to get some decent clothes, maybe do something with your hair . . ."

"I don't understand," She searched Julia's face. "What is it you want?"

"I told you, to help you."

"Why do you want to help me?"

Julia closed her eyes and forced her lips into a patient smile. "If you come with me right now, we can talk about it. You're going to have to trust me. You're going to have to be willing to take a chance." She was already getting up, but Dotty only continued to stare.

"I'm talking about right now," Julia said. She turned and headed out into the street.

Halfway to the car she heard the scuffle of Dotty's china-doll shoes try-ing to catch up. She caught Julia by the elbow.

"I could tell you weren't afraid to take chances," Julia said, smiling.

Vida took the back seat so that Dotty could sit up front. Julia fired the engine, but first gear wouldn't bite. She fought the gears into second and bumped out into traffic.

"I know it seems a little strange," Julia said, pushing her way towards the freeway, "but I could tell by the way you tracked me down that we have a sim-ilar way of getting things done," she said. "But you've got to be with me all the way. One shot. A package deal. Are you with me?"

"Where are we going? Why are we in such a hurry?"

"A friend of mine at the phone company owes me a favor. She's willing to see what kind of entry-level work she can find for you. You have an inter-view in thirty minutes."

Dotty gripped the seat with both hands. "Just like that? Look, lady, I was-
n't expecting anything like this. I don't know why you're doing this, but I'm
not so sure . . ."

A quick jab at the brakes sent Dotty reaching for the dashboard. A car
had cut in front of them without signaling.

"Is there any reason you can't start work tomorrow?" Julia said after a
minute.

"No," Dotty said. "But . . ."

Vida leaned forward against the seat and rested her chin on her fist.
"Better do what the boss says," she said. "It's useless to resist."

Noon-time traffic was heavier than Julia had expected. She dropped the
visor against the sun glaring off other cars. She fought traffic with swift lane
changes and alternate punches at the brakes and accelerator. She was afraid
that any break in rhythm of her plan would give the girl a chance to change
her mind.

Next to her, Dotty gnawed her thumbnail as she stared straight ahead. A
breeze through the partly opened window tousled her hair. To put her at ease
Julia said, "So tell me something about yourself. Where do you live? In the
Mission?"

"San Jose at 26."

"San Jose. How about that, Vida? That's your old street. What about your
brother? What kind of art does he do?"

The girl shrugged. "Everything," she said. "He's been drawing since he
was a kid. He starts school in August." Then a few minutes later she added,
"He won an award last month."

"And what about you? What plans do you have?"

She shrugged. "Maybe start my own business some day."

"That's terrific. Maybe we can help you with that. What do you say,
Vida?"

Vida looked out her window.

Julia kept asking questions. After a few minutes, Dotty said she was getting nervous and needed to use a bathroom. She wanted to fix her hair before
the interview. Julia pulled into the first gas station she saw and let Dotty out.

"I like her," Julia said, watching her disappear through the ladies room
door. "This is going to be the start of something new for us. I've never done
anything quite like this. Something important. Something real."

"Listen," Vida said, leaning forward. "I think this is a big mistake. We're
asking for trouble. We should take her back and forget the whole thing."

"Vida, what are you talking about? We're just getting started. Don't you see? We've been wasting our energy. This is our chance to do something that will last."

"The Art Institute doesn't open in August. It opens in September. Inés de la Cruz's daughter works there, so I know. I think she's lying to you, Julia."

"She probably just has the dates mixed up," Julia said.

"Yesterday, he's a kid with a little bit of talent and today he's winning awards? I don't believe it. I'll bet she's just some girlfriend he conned into helping him."

"You're jumping to conclusions," Julia said. "What do you have against her? Never mind. Here she comes." She got out of the car and slipped off her blazer. She held it out to Dotty. "Try this on. If it fits you can wear it to the interview." She stood back to get a full view. The blazer with the chinos and flat shoes was simple, but eye-catching.

Back in traffic, cars heading downtown were backed up to South Van Ness. Julia headed for the freeway on-ramp to bypass the congestion. She spiraled onto 80.

Dotty told about how she had waited nearly twenty minutes outside Marta's yesterday before coming in. "But then I figured I had nothing to lose," she said. She spoke more freely now, working quickly to fix her make-up in the vanity mirror.

"So tell me," Vida broke in. "What award did your brother win?"

She shrugged. "I don't remember what it was called."

"What did he win it for?" Vida said.

"A magazine cover he drew."

"How old is he?"

"Seventeen."

"What year was he born?"

Dotty hesitated, stopped applying make-up for a moment. "Sixty-six," she finally said.

Vida caught Julia's eye in the mirror. She leaned back very slowly and crossed her arms.

"Let's just concentrate on getting you to the interview," Julia said. "We can talk about your brother later."

"If there is anything we can do for him," Vida said. "They're really cracking down on kids these days, you know. Treating them as adults. Not giving them any special breaks."

"Vida!" Julia said.

"Well, it's true," Vida said. "Isn't that what the police told us?"

Dotty looked at her. "Is that true? Is what she's saying true?"

"No. Not necessarily," Julia said.

"You said you could do something," she said.

"I said I would try," Julia said. A stationwagon to her right was keeping her from changing lanes She gassed the Impala, but the other car edged forward next to her.

"I want to know," Dotty said. "Can you help him or not?"

"I'm going to do everything I can," she said. A car behind her flashed its lights for her to hurry up and pass. "I'm very good in these situations. Isn't that right, Vida?"

Vida crossed her legs in the back corner. She inspected her nails.

Julia brought the car past the speed limit, kept it rumbling there for several minutes.

Finally, Dotty turned to her. "Look," she said, "I don't think this is such a good idea. I think you should take me back. I want you to stop the car."

Julia held the gas pedal flush with the floor. The car started to shake, the mirror rattling the view behind her into a jagged blur. The stationwagon was still at her side.

"I mean it," Dotty said. "I shouldn't have listened to you. This is some kind of trick." She rattled the door handle. Her window suddenly dropped halfway down, letting in a rush of warm air. Her hair broke loose from its clasp and whirled around her face. "I want to get out. Pull off at the next exit. I want to get out now."

When Julia thought she had enough clearance, she cut into the next lane in front of the stationwagon. Dotty reached for the dashboard as the car swayed.

"You have to let me out," she said. "This is kidnapping."

"Please stay calm. Everything is going to be all right."

Dotty reached over and grabbed at the steering wheel. The car swerved a lane to the right. A car coming up fast behind blasted its horn and sped past.

"You never planned to do anything for my brother." She was breathing hard. She put a hand to her chest. She reached as if for her coat pocket. "My jacket," she said.

Julia saw an exit coming up. She fought her way towards the right lane, trying to make the off-ramp. She missed it. She pulled off the road instead, skidded to a stop in the gravel.

Dotty's face went pale. She pulled at her door handle.

"You can't get out that way." Julia jumped out and threw open the trunk. She fumbled through the girl's jacket. The girl was right behind her. She grabbed the inhaler from her, pressed it to her mouth, took a long breath. Color flowed back into her cheeks.

Julia put a hand on her back. "Tell me you're okay," she said. "Tell me you're okay."

Dotty leaned against the car, tipped her head to the sky. Her hair was plastered over her damp face in a criss-cross pattern. She nodded that she was all right.

"Thank God," Julia breathed.

After a few moments, Dotty shook off Julia's blazer and put on her bomber jacket. She hooked the blazer on the car's antenna and started walking.

"Wait a minute," Julia said. "You can still make this interview. We can still work together. I told you, there's a lot I can do for you." She watched her for several minutes until she had disappeared down the off-ramp they had just passed.

In the car, she set the hazard lights flashing, then spun in her seat to face Vida. "Why, Vida? What in the world were you thinking?"

"She was lying," she said.

"So what?" Julia said. "Think of what we might have accomplished."

"It was girls like that that used to make us miserable," she said. "Don't you remember? We promised we'd never let each other be taken advantage of. I couldn't let her do that to you. People rely on you, Julia."

Julia stepped out into the gravel, tried to figure out what to do. They were on an overpass that looked down over the southern part of the city. She tried to catch sight of the girl somewhere on the streets below. She might catch up with her if she hurried. But she had passed the nearest exit and there were no signs for another one as far as she could see.

She stood by the railing for a moment. A police car started to slow down for her, but she waved it on. The girl was all right, and she could always call her in a day or two and apologize for the way things went. She could reschedule the interview, or even find something for her at her real estate office. Yes, that's how she would handle it. Everything was fine, nothing had changed.

She leaned against the railing and caught her breath. A strong, spring wind blew up suddenly from below, tearing her hat away. In one deft, instinctive motion she reached dangerously far over the railing and caught it. The ground below swelled up towards her as she steadied her footing. She became dizzy as she realized how high up she was. She worked the edges of the hat with both hands. She pressed it tight against her heart, like a stop against the panic rising there.

FLORA IN SHADOWS

EVERY MORNING, RIDING THE CONCORD TRAIN to her downtown typing job, Alicia Núñez would check the *Tribune*'s obituaries for the name of her best friend's husband, Oscar Velásquez. When, after ten years, the name finally appeared, she got off the train at Lake Merrit and crossed the station to wait for a train home. At the edge of the platform she inspected the paper with her bifocals on, then without them at arm's length, then inches from her face. When she was certain that her eyes were not playing tricks on her, and somewhat certain that she was not dreaming, she surrendered to the fluttering of her heart. The man that for a decade had kept her from seeing her best friend was at last gone from this earth.

At home she called her office to say she would not be in for a few days. A corkscrew of bursitis pain in her left knee flared up as she climbed the attic steps, but she paid no attention to it. One by one she brought down the boxes of things she had been saving for Flora—ten years worth of newspaper clippings, crochet patterns, gardening magazines, and packets of the exotically colored flower seeds that her friend, color-blind to all but the most violent hues, had been fond of growing.

In the last box she found a photo from the last time they had been together—Oscar and Flora, and Mauricio and herself—crowded around a Marina picnic table on the Fourth of July, faces lit red with beer and laughter. They had been *comadres* and *compadres,* friends as close as family members, people who saw you through every crisis, shared the responsibilities of raising your children, and ate from your table, heartily and without reservation, as you were expected to eat from theirs. They had shared keys to each others' homes, taken every vacation together, and spent every summer weekend in the protection of one or the other's shaded brick patio.

It had been that way until the morning Alicia called Flora for their usual chat as they fried their husbands' breakfasts of eggs and steak. They had been talking for just a few minutes when Flora suddenly snipped the conversation short. "Well, I have to go. I'll call you later."

The next morning there had been no answer at all. Alicia did not reach her until late in the afternoon. Again, Flora said she was too busy to talk.

"Tell me what's wrong, *Coma*. Did I say something to offend you?"

"Oh, no, it's nothing, *Comadre*," Flora's voice edged into its highest register. "Listen, I have *chiles* on the stove, we'll talk later."

"I can't figure out what's wrong with the *comadre*," she told Mauricio later. He was hunched over his drill press in the garage, his slender arms stippled with pine shavings from a cabinet he was making. "Has the *compadre* said anything to you?"

From the washroom doorway where she stood she saw his back coil tight. "How should I know?" he said. "Is it my responsibility to track their every move? We spend too much time with those people as it is."

That was when she knew that the men had been fighting. Never before had Mauricio referred to the Velásquezes except in the most affectionate of terms—never as "those people." She suspected the rift between the men had to do with the fact that she and Mauricio had recently begun talking about divorce. Oscar was a devout Catholic and considered those who could not stand by their vows to be cowards. But more than this, he would have seen their divorce as a betrayal, not only of the Church, but of the family the four of them had spent so many years creating. Whatever the reason, Oscar apparently had forbidden Flora to talk to the "enemy camp." Flora was devoted to Oscar, and there was no point in trying to talk to her until things blew over. Oscar had a violent temper, and Alicia did not want to cause trouble for her friend. Months later, after she and Mauricio did divorce, Alicia showed up on the Velásquez's doorstep to talk to Flora. Oscar placed himself squarely in the doorway. Without explanation, he told her never to come by again.

※ ※ ※

Alicia waited until a few days after the funeral to visit Flora. She would go by unannounced, as she had often done in the old days. She thought about having her hair done in a new way, but thought better of it. She wanted to appear as Flora would remember her, her hair permed simply, wearing a sleeveless house dress that did not hide the plumpness of her arms. She wanted nothing to get in the way of picking up where they'd left off.

At the station she bought a warm copy of the *Tribune* and out of habit turned to the obituaries. When she realized what she was doing, she began laughing so hard that tears began to pearl in the corners of her eyes. She gave the paper away to a man in a wool coat.

That morning the train thudded slowly over the tracks. Gray industrial buildings floated by, silent, ghostlike. Alicia's heart beat quickly. She fidgeted with her purse strap until it broke. The bursitis in her knee, caused by a car accident fifteen years earlier, was especially bad that day. Her doctor had told her to avoid walking whenever the swelling became visible. But when she got to the Oakland station, she was too agitated to wait for the bus. She began the two mile walk to Flora's house.

Alicia recognized Flora's street by a colonnade of winter-stricken trees. But much else in the neighborhood had changed. Competitively maintained hedges and geometric rock gardens that had been put in during the drought years had been paved over or abandoned to weeds. Time and neglect had blistered the exteriors of once-quaint wood-paneled houses, and although the neighborhood was as quiet as she remembered it, the quality of that quiet had changed. It was no longer the quiet of peacefulness, but of desolation.

By the time she got to Flora's house, she found herself hoping Flora had moved away. She did not want to think of her living amidst such dinginess. Only now did she think that Flora, too, might have changed for the worse. Her heart pounded as she went up the steps. For the first time, she thought perhaps she shouldn't have come.

But the tall, gangly woman in the white robe who answered the door was the Flora she remembered. Her face, framed by an arc of yellow curlers, reminded Alicia of a half-plucked daisy. Her quizzical expression trembled on the slender, nervous stem of her neck as she peered at Alicia through the mesh.

"Don't tell me you've lost all your manners since I last saw you," Alicia said. "Well, don't just stand there. Invite your old *coma* in."

Flora pushed the screen open for her, then drew back, put her hands over her mouth. "My God. *Comadre. Alicia.*"

She hovered there for a minute, her mouth agape, fish-like. Then she started flying about the room, straightening furniture and pulling up blinds and grabbing loose clothes that kept spilling out of her arms.

"*Coma,* had I known . . . the place is in such . . . I haven't had a chance to . . . if I had expected . . ."

"Please," Alicia said, "don't trouble yourself. I should have called first. I wanted to surprise you."

Flora's rubbery fingers flew to her hair and started plucking curlers.

Alicia took her forearm and stopped her. "Please," she said softly. She lead her to the sofa, sat down across from her on the coffee table.

Alicia took Flora's hands in hers and looked at her. Big, moist eyes danced behind Flora's thick glasses. Springs of black and silver curls sprouted wildly from the uncurlered side of her head.

"All these years," Flora breathed.

"We have time to catch up now," Alicia said.

"You heard about Oscar?"

"I read it in the paper."

"I should have called you."

"You had no reason to."

"If you only knew. . ."

"There's nothing to explain."

"How you must hate me."

"Don't talk nonsense."

Alicia searched Flora's worried face. Time had deepened the lines around her eyes, her mouth, but the long, delicate bones of her face were as charming as ever.

"Oh, it's good to see you again," Flora said. She wiped her nose, then got up and laughed. "I must look ridiculous." She shuffled to the bathroom in her slippers.

"Really, Flora," Alicia called out. "I'm so sorry about Oscar. Did you know Mauricio and I finally divorced? Just a few months after I last saw you."

There was no answer from the bathroom. Alicia got up and walked through the rest of the house where the four of them had spent so much time together. Army photos of Flora's son, Miguel, still hung above the TV cabinet and the same knitted cushions were angled in the corners of the sofa. But somehow, instead of reassuring her, these details troubled Alicia. Everything was too much the same, as if time had stalled for Flora, while Alicia's own life had continued to move forward.

In the kitchen she opened the refrigerator, but it was almost empty. She found some lemons on the counter, which she cut and squeezed into glasses, adding water and then sugar from a chipped porcelain jar. She brought the glasses into the living room.

"We have a lot of catching up to do," Alicia said when Flora came out. "Tell me about Miguel. Are he and Melissa still in Phoenix?"

Flora said that her son had finally married Melissa after six years and that Melissa had given birth to twins, one of which had nearly died from pneumonia. They talked for a long while, spinning freely back and forth through the years, weaving in life's details since they had last seen each other.

"We're going to have such good times together again," Alicia said.

Flora smiled, but her eyes glimmered with tears. Her smile began to quake.

"I'm so sorry," Alicia said. "It's rude of me to talk this way so soon after the *compa* died."

Flora wiped her eyes and nose. "You don't know how it is, *Coma.*"

"I know it's hard to lose him."

"That's not what I mean." She stood, folded her arms as if against a chill as she paced. "Things are pretty bad right now. I'm going to have to sell the house. There's no way I can make the mortgage payments."

"What about the *compa?*" Alicia said.

"He didn't leave much."

"Insurance?"

"He couldn't get any with his heart condition."

Alicia felt something simmer inside her. "Can't Miguel help you?"

"They already have two mortgages. He's promised to come out and take care of selling the house for me. I wouldn't know where to start."

Alicia tried to stay calm, but her anger spilled over, infecting her words. "What was Oscar thinking? He knew he was at risk. He should have been preparing for the worst. And you, what are you going to do? Where will you go?"

Flora shrugged. "I'm going to go live with Miguel. They're both working. They could use the help with the little ones."

"Oh, that's just fine," Alicia snorted. "So you can spend another ten years raising kids. That's a fine inheritance."

Flora shrugged. "It's not so bad."

Not so bad. That was how she used to describe life with Oscar after one of his fits of anger, or the time she had suspected him of cheating on her with another woman. They had both looked the other way. It was just the way men were, they had been taught. Women just had to put up with it. But in return for these concessions, the men were supposed to see to it that their wives were taken care of, even after their deaths.

Alicia slowly began massaging her knee. "Don't worry," she said. "We'll figure something out. I swear to God. We'll figure something out."

❦ ❦ ❦

At home that night she studied her bank statements under the stark light of her kitchen lamp. She had enough money in savings to help Flora keep her house. But she could not give away her life's security. Since her divorce, her draw on this money together with her wages from her morning job had given her a freedom that both frightened and excited her. She had learned to make all her own decisions and to trust her ability to make them. Her life may not have seemed very interesting, compared to the way younger women were living their lives today, but for someone whose only work had been raising a child and taking care of a husband, it had been like a step into an exciting, foreign world. Her independence was the one thing she would not place at risk.

She stayed up late thinking, until the only solution that remained was the one that had been nipping at the edges of her consciousness all along. Flora would have to move in with her.

Together they could live as cheaply as one. How many times, after all, had Alicia wished that they could have had more time together, just the two of them? How many times had they had to alter their weekend plans or end a conversation in order tend to a husband's desire or bruised ego? The men had come first, and because of this, she and Flora had always known each other as wives rather than as women.

The next morning, she went into Mauricio's old room and tried to imagine it as Flora's. Outside, a shifting of clouds caused the room to lighten as if with approval. The whole house seemed to breathe with the hope of new possibilities.

"It's a lovely thought," Flora said when she asked her. "You're much too generous. I couldn't take advantage of you that way."

At first Alicia was willing to leave it at that, but the more she thought about it, the more sense living together made. There were chores that were becoming harder for Alicia to do because of her knee that Flora could help with, like waxing the floors, or kneeling to clean the tub. In a few years, Alicia knew she would have to move in with her daughter, Ana, who lived in Colorado. She loved Ana, but did not want to move to Colorado. She wanted to hold onto independence as long as she could.

"You'd be doing me a favor," she insisted when she called again.

"It's too soon for me," Flora said.

"I can't stand the thought of you in that neighborhood."

"It's not so bad."

"You shouldn't be alone."

"Miguel will be here."

It took six calls to convince her. Finally, she agreed to move in once Miguel had come to arrange the sale of her house. Two months later, Flora arrived in her son's pickup. It was loaded high with trunks and boxes.

"The first thing I want to do," Flora said once they had brought everything in, "is to get my hands dirty. I can't stand to go a day without gardening."

Alicia gave her the seeds and bulbs she had been saving, and Flora went to work tearing up the neglected back yard. From the kitchen window, Alicia could see her pulling down dead vines from the back fence and forcefully turning up the hardened beds around the patio. She bundled the vines and hacked at weeds with a violence that made Alicia hold her breath. Once or twice she thought she saw Flora crying.

Alicia went into Mauricio's room—Flora's room now—to help unpack. She came across Flora's wedding picture in a suitcase. Oscar's broad, boastful grin contrasted with Flora's barely perceptible smile. She went to the linen closet to wipe the dust from it, and as she did, Oscar kept smiling at her. Impulsively, she pushed the picture to the back of the closet. Later, when Flora asked if she had seen it, Alicia pretended not to hear the question.

That night, they stayed up after dinner talking at the kitchen table. They did not move to clear away dishes, or clean the stove, or turn off the lights in the rest of the house. They talked. Conversation flowed out around them in continuous ribbons of nostalgia. Only when Alicia touched on the topic of Oscar's death was there silence. Then the life in Flora's wide eyes flickered out, and her shoulders heaved thickly.

Alicia asked Flora to meet her downtown the next day for lunch, and afterwards they stopped to open a checking account that they could both use for buying groceries and things for the garden and house. Back at Alicia's office, her head spinning from the beers she had with lunch, Alicia introduced Flora to the other women she worked with.

Flora continued to tackle everything she did with an aggression that made Alicia nervous. Throughout the house she rearranged furniture daily, loudly thumping the heavy pieces around by herself. She tore apart old flower beds, pounded them together in new configurations. And for hours every afternoon the garage came alive with the whir of Mauricio's old electric saws and drills and the thunder of hammers on wood as Flora rebuilt storage units for the pantry so that Alicia would not have to risk hurting her knee by using a step ladder. Alicia kept out of her way. This was Flora's way of coping with Oscar's death, and Alicia was convinced that her aggression was directed at him.

One night Alicia woke to see Flora's face floating over her like a pale, quivering moon. "Alicia," she was saying. "Wake up. I think there's someone in the back yard."

"It's just the neighbor's cat getting into the trash again," Alicia murmured. She pulled the sheets to her chin, but Flora shook the bedframe.

"Please, Alicia. Do something."

Alicia got up and padded to the kitchen with Flora behind her. She opened the porch door, and when she flicked on the light, a cat flashed topaz eyes at them, then leapt down silently from the fence. "What did I tell you?" Alicia said.

She went back to bed, but woke an hour later to find Flora sitting in a chair across from her. "What is it this time?" Alicia groaned, flicking on the light.

"I'm sorry. I'm too nervous to sleep. I've been like this ever since Oscar died. If you'd just let me sit here with you for a few minutes . . ."

"Well, now I'm not going to be able to sleep either," Alicia said, throwing the covers down with annoyance.

"I'm sorry," Flora said. "Wait. I know." She left the room and came back with a bottle of cherry brandy and two small plastic glasses. "This will help."

She slid under the covers next to Alicia and poured out a whisper of liquor for each of them. The sweet cherry-flavored liquid went down smoothly, and in a few minutes, they were again lost in conversation. When sleep finally snagged Alicia, it pulled her down into a deep, rich dream.

Sleeping in the same bed became habit. Each night Flora would appear with brandy, and they would talk for long stretches, mostly about the times they used to spend together. At times, Alicia would act annoyed at being kept up, but in fact she was sleeping better than she had in years, and, at night at least, the ache in her leg became little more than a ghost of what it once was.

One night after they had had a little more brandy than usual, Flora asked, "Why did you divorce Mauricio?"

The question surprised Alicia, for she thought she had already explained this to Flora several times. "We had grown too far apart," she told her again. "We argued for the first twenty-five years, and then one day we just stopped—stopped arguing, stopped talking, stopped everything. We were pretending to be married."

"Was there another woman?"

"No, no, nothing like that."

"Did he ever hurt you?"

"Of course not."

"Well," Flora said, "then I don't understand. You seemed happy." She took a long sip of brandy, shook her head.

"Didn't you ever think about leaving Oscar?" Alicia ventured. "He had such a terrible temper. How did you put up with it?"

Flora shrugged, poured a little more brandy. She frowned into her glass.

"He kept us apart for ten years," Alicia said. "Doesn't that make you angry?"

"He did the best he could," was all Flora would say.

"Oscar's gone," Alicia said. "You're not betraying him by talking about him."

But Flora only got up to use the bathroom, and when she came back said she was not in a mood to talk and turned out the light.

✿✿ ✿✿ ✿✿

At the end of their first month together, Alicia found they had exceeded their monthly budget by two hundred dollars. The extra expense of having Flora there and of restarting the garden explained the discrepancy, but it did not ease the crimp she felt in her stomach as she revised her budget upward for the next month.

"We'll be more careful this month," Flora said, when Alicia mentioned it. "As soon as my house is sold I can pay you back for everything. You don't have anything to worry about."

As April slipped by, Alicia realized that life with Flora was going to continue to be more expensive than she had guessed. Wherever had she gotten the notion that two could live as cheaply as one? Certainly that had not been the case with Mauricio, who had to have expensive T-bones and fillets twice a week. Flora, too, had her luxuries, like her cherry brandy, Mexican glamour magazines, and crochet yarn for her hobbies.

The afternoon Alicia planned to talk to her about these things, she came home to find that Flora had gone to bed early. The house was warm with the scent of a pepper-stuffed round steak. In the kitchen Flora had left her a plate warming in the oven. She ate the steak, then went into the bathroom to soak her leg in a cold bath and found that Flora had installed handles above the tub for Alicia to hold onto. A slow burn of shame spread across Alicia's face. Mauricio had always accused her of being cheap, and for the first time in her life she truly felt she was. The few dollars she was losing each month were nothing compared with everything Flora brought into her life. The next time she went to the bank, she transferred a thousand dollars into their account to cover extra expenses.

❧ ❧ ❧

Late in May the first shoots of petunias, marigolds, and nemesia began poking through the soil in the garden. It had been five years since Alicia had been able to work the yard, and she felt great pleasure to be able to look out each morning at these tiny signs of life. Flora continued to maintain the yard, but there was less for her to do now. When an early heat wave descended on the Bay Area, Flora started spending her days indoors with the drapes drawn to block out the heat. She started rising later and spent much of her time paging through her magazines and beginning crochet projects that she never seemed to finish. Alicia came home one afternoon to find her sitting on the sofa in the shadows of the unlit living room, still in her night gown, her feet curled under her, a glass with an inch of brandy in it cupped in her lap. She blinked blearily as Alicia opened the curtains. Flora had been crying.

Alicia went to the hall closet to find the albums where she saved pictures of past holidays. She thought looking at them might be a way to get Flora to talk about Oscar and start dealing with her loss. But as she turned the pages, she noticed an odd thing. There did not seem to be any good photos of her friend. In one, her face was obscured by Oscar's waving hand. In another she had moved half out of the camera's range, and in another she was blurred beyond recognition by a sudden movement. In every picture, though she hovered taller than everyone else, she was behind the others, her weak smile obscured by the shadows in which she stood.

That Alicia had never noticed this before for some reason shook her deeply. She put the photos away and did not show them to Flora.

"You need to get out more," she told Flora. She heard herself speaking more firmly than she had ever spoken to Flora before, her words driven by a fear she did not understand. "You should think about finding some work. It would be good for you."

"Oh, no," she said. "I have plenty to do here. I have my projects. I have the garden."

"You need to be around people more," Alicia persisted, "not cooped up in here all day. It's not healthy."

"Well," Flora said, "maybe you're right. I'll think about getting out more." She forced up a smile, took a sip of brandy, and went back to crocheting.

❧ ❧ ❧

Three days later, two gleaming fire trucks were pulled into Alicia's driveway when she came home. Two men in black and yellow uniforms were dragging hoses to the truck, and a scattering of neighbors with arms folded stood watching from the sidewalk across the street. Over the house a wisp of black smoke drifted against the flat blue. Alicia rushed past the trucks towards the house, but one of the firemen stepped in front of her.

"Is this your house?"

"What happened?" she said, trying to get past him. "Where's Flora?"

He told her to stay calm and lead her to the other side of the truck, where Flora was sitting in the grass with her legs straight out in front of her like a child. Her dirtied house dress was spread all around her, and her smoke-blackened face was streaked by tears that had long since dried. She looked up at her, blinking stupidly.

"Oh my God, Flora, are you okay?"

"I had oil heating on the stove for *churros,*" Flora said sheepishly. "I guess I forgot about it and fell asleep in the living room."

Alicia found the kitchen window smashed where firemen had forced their way in. The rose-pattern wallpaper was black from smoke and a quarter inch of gray water covered the floor. Water had seeped into the living room and down the hall, too, soaking all the wool rugs and runners. From the side table next to the sofa a brandy bottle and glass glinted at her.

Repairs to the kitchen and replacing the stove and the rugs cost Alicia nearly two thousand dollars. By the time her next bank statement arrived, she had depleted a third of her savings, and was still losing a little more each month. The more time she spent looking for places to save, the more her knee bothered her. Twice at work she found herself so distracted by thoughts of money that she starting typing without feeding paper through the carriage. When Flora prepared a meal of rack of lamb to celebrate seven months together, all Alicia could think about was how expensive the lamb must have been, how unnecessary the wine that went with it.

Flora still spent most of her days indoors, even though the garden had exploded in a riot of summer colors. Aggressive red and yellow marigolds burst open in the planters along the patio, and disorderly masses of nasturtium crashed with drifts of petunias and hyacinths in a way that Alicia found unsettling. The angry colors seemed to yell at her, and she found herself keeping the kitchen windows drawn so she would not have to look at them. But most disturbing of all was the fact that the brighter the garden grew, the more sapped Flora became, as if her flowers were drawing their strength directly from her.

"You must get a job," Alicia told her one evening. "You can't go on living like this. And you know we really could use the money."

She got her an application from the plant nursery down the street. She had seen a HELP WANTED sign in the window and could not imagine a place Flora would enjoy working more. The contact with people and the fresh air would do her wonders.

The morning Flora had promised to talk to the manager, she called Alicia at her office. Her voice quaked through the line's static.

"I don't know about this, Alicia. I haven't worked since Oscar . . ."

"Don't think about Oscar," she said. "You're going to be fine. Do you have the application?"

"I spilled coffee on it."

"You don't drink coffee."

"I feel sick."

"Take some Pepto."

"I feel dizzy. My English, Alicia. Why would they hire me?"

"You have plenty of things going for you."

"What do I have going for me?"

"I don't know," she snapped, but caught herself. "Listen, you'll be fine. I can't talk now."

Never before had she felt such irritation towards her friend. But, she reminded herself, neither had she ever seen her before out of the shadow of her husband. Flora was like one of her sun-hungry marigolds, which left too long in the shade fails to flower. Alicia recalled how after her divorce the very air around her had taken on a nourishing quality. She had felt her spirit shifting, edging out of its old self and into a new shape. That's what Flora needed: to be brought out of the shadows and into a place where she could thrive.

"I don't know what I was so nervous about," Flora said that night. "The man at the nursery was very nice. I'll be able to bring home starters for just pennies."

The week passed, and Flora did not mention the job again. When Alicia went by the nursery the following week, the HELP WANTED was still in the window.

She tried again several more times that month to persuade her to look for work, but hardly knew what advice to give her. Alicia's own job she had gotten almost by accident, through a clerk at the corner store whose son ran the

typing pool in Oakland. In the meantime, Alicia watched her savings continue to dwindle, approaching the teller every other Friday with a knotted feeling
in her stomach.

✿ ✿ ✿

Her first thoughts of asking Flora to move out came just as the November
nights were beginning to leave a rime of frost on the windows. It made her
dizzy to imagine how she would tell her, but there was nothing else she could
do. She could no longer enjoy Flora's company without reservation, could no
longer bear the melancholy air that filled the house and seemed to cling to her
skin long after she left the house every day. She weighed these thoughts over
and over, trying to choose the gentlest words she could think of.

But she had hardly convinced herself that she was doing the right thing,
when Flora swept into the bedroom one morning while Alicia was dressing.
Flora's nightgown was aflutter, her cheeks flushed with excitement.

"Miguel just sold the house," she said. "He's already accepted an offer."

Alicia felt all the tension run out of her body like a river escaping through
a sluice. She hugged her friend long and hard. Out of bleak, ashen thoughts,
the life she had originally seen for them remolded itself in her imagination.

They celebrated over dinner with several glasses of wine. For the first
time in weeks they talked long into the night, unraveling the same old stories
of family, laughing at the same jokes and mishaps of their youth. Alicia talked
about someday taking a vacation, just the two of them, perhaps to someplace
tropical where flowers grew in colors more brilliant than anything Flora had
ever seen before. But as the night wore on, Alicia learned that the sale of the
house might not go through for months. There were still roofing and foundation inspections to be done, and it was still possible that the buyers would
change their minds, withdraw, lose interest.

Alicia began to wake up each day pestered by the same old uncertainties.
She thought of asking her daughter for money, but it was still too early for
that. At the office she asked if there was any extra work she could take on. She
would feel better if she could at least keep an even keel financially until Flora
got her money. But the typing pool was overstaffed for that time of year, and
it would be months before there would be more for her to do.

On her way home she remembered the nursery job she had tried to convince Flora to take.

The sign was still in the window when she got there. The owner, a tall,
slow-talking bearded man with desperate eyes that frightened her told her that

he needed someone to run the cash register in the late afternoons and sometimes on weekends. The job paid half of what her typing job did, but she
accepted it eagerly. He did not ask her to fill out an application, and she started that same day.

The room she worked in smelled heavily of pesticides and fertilizer, and
gave her a headache the moment she walked in. The owner showed her how
to run the register and the pricing sheets and how to handle deliveries when
he wasn't there. She did not like the way his hand settled on her shoulder as
he showed her how to fill out a sales receipt.

Customers expected her to know much more than she did about plant
nutrition and perennials and garden pests. She tried to remember things that
Flora had taught her, but often found herself realizing long after a customer
had left that she had told him the wrong way to prune a rose or how frequently
to water a ficus. She rarely had an opportunity to sit down, and the stress
caused her knee to ache worse than ever. Flora would have been much better
at this job, and she could not understand why she had not shown more interest in it. She doubted whether she had come in for the interview at all. Every
day Alicia came home so tired from working two jobs that she was determined
to quit the nursery. But every second Friday, her account inching back up was
like a balm to all her problems, and she would go back to work on Monday,
having forgotten all about how exhausted she had been Friday.

She saw little of Flora over the next few weeks. Now that there wasn't
much to be done in the yard, she could not imagine how Flora was spending
her days. But at the same time, she really didn't want to know. At the end of
each day, she was either too tired or ached too much to spend time with her.

Her knee continued to worsen, a hot blossom of pain opening up more
and more each day. On the day of the first of the winter rains, she almost could
not get out of bed. She decided to stay home with an ice pack that Flora
replaced every half hour. It was good to have her there to make her fresh fish
broth and to walk to the drugstore for her prescription of pain medication. But
in Alicia's heart gratefulness and resentment dwelt close by. Often when Flora
came into the room, Alicia pretended to be asleep so she would not have to
talk to her. Eight days went by before the pain subsided, and in that time she
lost as much money in wages as she had hoped to have saved.

She went back to work eagerly, taking on more hours at the nursery, and
working an occasional weekend. She was feeling rested now, and wanted to
take advantage of her energy before it faded. That she rarely saw Flora any-

more hardly bothered her. It was good to focus at last on making money without distraction.

One day while kneeling to move a flat of peonies for a customer, she felt the earth suddenly growing hot beneath her, as if she had been kneeling on a hotplate that someone had just plugged into a socket. She set down the flat. It was her bursitis, she was certain, but the pain subsided as soon as she stood up. Cautiously she took a step. No pain. She waited. Still no pain. Then a slight tingling. Then, slowly, fingers of heat wrapping around her knee, tightening their grip until the pain, at once hot and icy, became like an unutterable scream. She grabbed the counter to support herself, saw her own tears splattering on the formica. She barely heard her own words as she called for help.

One of her co-workers drove her to the emergency room at Oakland Kaiser, where a doctor with stifled breathing would not release her. X-rays showed her bursa, just below the knee-cap, swollen to the size of an egg. The trauma was severe enough that he chose to call an orthopedic specialist right away. She was checked into the hospital that night and scheduled for surgery the next morning.

She called Flora and told her what had happened, but did not mention the surgery, only that she was being kept for observation and would call tomorrow when she knew more. There was no point in upsetting her, she told herself, but in reality she did not want her to come to the hospital. She wanted time to think.

Hours passed, with nurses appearing at her bedside to take her blood pressure and give her pills; never the same nurse twice, it seemed. Finally, alone in the stark white room, she picked at the loose threads of her gown as she tried to retrace the mistakes that had landed her here, swathed in discomfort and uncertainty, alone in a sterile room, with only a couple of thousand dollars to her name. The doctors could not tell her when she would be able to work again. Maybe in a couple of months, maybe five, maybe six. She thought of calling Ana to let her know what had happened, but she knew she would fly out at once and would insist on staying with her and then taking her to Colorado. And if she went to Colorado, she believed she might give in and not come back. She wanted to hold on, even if for just a little while longer.

At eight in the evening, another nurse came in to give her her painkillers and sleeping pills. The drugs began to take effect quickly, but she resisted sleep. She did not want to drift off this way, with her thoughts in a jumble, her life out of control. She wanted to know what her next step would be when she woke up. In her state of exhaustion, she imagined her problems swirling about her in the form of small white spheres, like the numbers in a bingo cage. She tried to grasp them, to order them in some way, but there were too many of them and they moved too fast.

Around her, shadows were beginning to gather in the corners of the room. They edged their way towards her, a soft, creeping dimness filling up more and more of the space around her, encroaching. They seemed to be taking up the very air she was breathing. She tried to push them back, to hold them off long enough to make sense of things. But the lull of the medication was too seductive. At last, her mind and body relaxed. She surrendered to the tide of its influence, and everything around her went black.

❧ ❧ ❧

After her surgery, Alicia awoke in a pale blue room with an evenness of mind that surprised her, as if the surgery had removed her problems along with the egg-shaped swelling. Her calmness seemed to have an effect on Flora, too, when she arrived. There was none of the usual anxiousness in Flora's voice, no wringing of hands or nervous pacing or frantic-fingered gestures as Alicia told her that living together probably would not work anymore. Flora merely smiled sadly and ran the back of her hand over Alicia's forehead and down her cheek, as if to say, "Don't worry. I know it's best. I'll go."

Flora came to the hospital the next day, bringing Alicia fresh fruit and homemade sandwiches and Spanish magazines. She stayed only for a few minutes, and they talked very little. When Alicia was able to come home, she found that Flora had moved back into her own room.

A great sadness hung in the air of the house for the next few weeks. The days were getting shorter, the sun peaking low in the sky just long enough to cast a few weak shadows through the house. Flora continued to care for her, cooking and helping her change her dressings, refilling prescriptions, and helping her up on her crutches when she needed to use the bathroom. But Alicia could also feel her keeping a measured distance as she arranged to join her daughter-in-law in Phoenix and have her things shipped. With so much planning to do, Flora became more directed in her energies, more steady of nerve. Alicia felt she was beginning to see her friend clearly for the first time, as if the frantic blur that had always been Flora was finally standing still enough that a camera could capture her true self.

The news that escrow had closed on Flora's house came during the last week of winter, just as Flora was preparing the garden for spring. After she had finished speaking with Miguel, she called to reserve her ticket for Phoenix.

Now that the house was sold, Alicia once again began to wonder: Was there really any reason for Flora not to stay? She was seeing a change in her, a sign that she might emerge into a new life the two of them could share. But no, she had to tell herself, no. She had taken all the risks she was willing to take. Flora was still living in a shadowy realm from which Alicia did not believe she had the strength or the ingenuity to rescue her.

By Flora's last day, Alicia was walking without crutches again and was able to help her pack the last of her things. It seemed to take much longer than it had to unpack, as if her possessions resisted the very process. Flora went out of the bedroom to find a bedcover she had begun knitting but never finished. When she did not come back, Alicia went to look for her and found her crumpled into the sofa. A segment of the bedcover had unraveled down her legs and across the living room floor. Alicia sat down next to her.

"It's not going to be so bad. We'll still be able to visit each other. The desert is supposed to be beautiful."

Flora tried to control her sobbing. A scent of cherries filled the air around her.

"I know it's difficult, but you can't keep this up. You have to get over Oscar."

"So many years," Flora said. "It's all my fault, all my fault."

"Please don't blame yourself," Alicia said. "You were doing what you thought you had to do, what Oscar told you to do."

She shook her head. "Oscar never made me do anything. It was my decision to break ties with you. The day you came to the house, I asked Oscar to send you away."

Alicia stared at her. She reached for Flora's hands, but they were balled tightly into fists.

"Why?" Alicia said.

"I thought you were being so selfish," she said. "I was furious with you, but I couldn't face you. Mauricio was a better husband to you than Oscar ever was to me. It wasn't fair. It just wasn't fair."

"Why didn't you say anything? I would have understood."

"I thought I was over all of that. When you asked me to stay here I thought it was my chance to make things up to you. But now I've made a mess of this too."

Alicia tried to reassure her, but the overlapping webs of pain and confusion on Flora's face left her feeling more powerless than ever. She could not think of anything to say.

She heard Miguel's truck pull into the driveway. There was a light tap on the horn, then a door slam and Miguel was at the door. She let him in, and he helped carry Flora's bags to the curb. She hugged Flora, smelled the brandy again. She could not help feeling that she had failed her in ways she had been unaware of. But as the truck carrying Flora and her possessions rounded the corner out of sight, she also felt a wave of relief. Guilt was buoyed away by relief.

✽✽✽ ✽✽✽ ✽✽✽

Alicia was welcomed back to work with an enthusiasm that took her by surprise. She had been worried that her job might be in jeopardy, but a flu had swept through the office at the busiest time of year, making her indispensable. A card signed by the other employees and potted daisies were waiting for her on her desk when she arrived, and when her boss insisted on taking her to lunch, he could not stop saying how happy he was that she was back.

She threw herself into her work with greater vigor than at any time since Flora had moved in. The gratitude and praise from her boss lifted her emotions, made her realize how blunted her spirit had become in the last few months. It felt good, too, to work without physical pain. Her surgery had left her feeling better than she had since her accident, and the doctors told her that as long as she did not exert herself too much and did the prescribed exercises with care, she could go without discomfort for many years to come.

From time to time Alicia would be overcome by sadness as she thought of her last moments with Flora. She had seen a side of her friend so unexpected she had not known how to react to it, and it troubled her greatly to think she still understood her so little after so much time. It was as if an unexpected shifting of clouds had lit up an angle of her friend's character that she hadn't known existed, then just as quickly had shifted back, not giving her time to put words to what she had seen.

Alicia thought about calling Flora, but wasn't sure what she would say. It did not surprise her that she had heard from Flora only once since she had moved out. She knew Flora would have to endure another long, emotionally turbulent period before anyone would be able to coax her back into her life.

Every day she found reasons to put off calling Flora. She did not want to jinx the new course her own life was taking.

In May, Alicia thought she might begin working on the garden herself. She hated to think it should revert to the way it was before Flora had arrived. Many of the seeds and bulbs Flora had planted had already come up, and to these Alicia added zinnias and begonias and geraniums, working just a few minutes each afternoon so as not to strain herself. She got to work on a thorough spring cleaning as well. With Flora gone, dust had begun to settle over everything, and the windows still carried a residue of winter grime. While she was sorting out the linen closet, she came across the wedding picture she had hidden from Flora the day she had moved in. She flushed all at once with shame. Had she really done this childish thing? Suddenly she missed Flora terribly and decided to call her for a long talk.

She set the picture on the mantle as a reminder to do so later in the week. But every time she came across it, she was so ashamed of herself that she put off calling for another day. Finally, she got tired of looking at it and put the picture out of sight and forgot about it.

A few weeks later Alicia received a check in the mail from Flora for three thousand dollars. She had never expected Flora to pay her back. She decided to call her that same day to thank her, but also to tell her that she was doing fine and no longer needed the money. She would return the check to her. She got out her address book and dialed Miguel's number in Phoenix.

The prerecorded voice on the line told her that the number had been disconnected. She dialed it again, then called Phoenix information. "I'm sorry," the operator told her. "I don't see a number for that name."

She tried again, using Melissa's name, Flora's married name, Flora's maiden name, but there were no listings. She sat for a long time trying to figure out what to do. Certainly Flora wouldn't have moved without telling her. Yet, Flora had once gone ten years without contacting her; who was Alicia to say she would not just as easily go another ten or more?

In the middle of the night she remembered the last name of one of Miguel's neighbors in Phoenix. She called information and asked for every number for the name Adler, then called each one until she reached the right person, a man named Luis.

"They moved away," the voice told her. "No, no, no. I don't know where they moved to."

"Do you know who might know?"

"Not at all. Hardly ever talked to them. Noisy bunch of kids."

"Please try to remember," Alicia said. "Call me if you remember anything."

She tried to recall other names, other friends of Flora's. But she had been Flora's only friend in all the time she had known her. She blamed herself all the more for having failed her. But Flora might still call. She would call when she was ready. She would send a card to say where she was.

Weeks passed without word from Flora, and Alicia began to think less and less about her. She was working almost full-time, and now that her knee was better, she did not mind the longer hours. The loss of her friendship still lingered at the edges of her mind, but her life was good and enjoyable and she was for the most part happy to leave things the way they were.

One day she stepped out into the garden and saw sprouts from the last of the bulbs Flora had planted pushing their way through the soil in places throughout the yard that Alicia did not know had been planted. She was surprised at the number of them, how they had thrived without being tended to. She wanted to believe that Flora, too, was doing all right, wherever she was. She went back into the house and went on with her day.

As Alicia began to take on more work, she again found she had little time to take care of the yard. Still, each morning, she would look out at the garden as she poured her coffee and wonder at how well the flowers were doing. She knew from the year before that the flowers—zinnias, marguerites, begonias, and marigolds, in their unreal shades of red and orange and brilliant yellow— would last long into the summer. On some days, when the morning was still overcast, the flowers would not yet have their faces fully open to the sky. At other times, they leapt at her in all their colors, disturbing as one of Flora's moods, insistent as an accusation.

THE KING OF SNOW

THE FIRST TIME I SAW A GRAM OF COCAINE at Stanford, it was on its way up the nose of Megan Barnett, the wealthiest girl in the freshman class of 1988. If that name sounds familiar, it's because her father, Wilson Barnett, was on trial at the time for his role in the biggest insider trading scandal of the decade. Every front page in the country was running daily trial updates with pictures of the heavy-set investment banker flanked by stone-faced attorneys.

I had just walked into Megan's room to see her hunched over a gilt-framed mirror with a straw to her nose, her blonde hair held back with a manicured hand, silver rings on every finger. She zipped a line up each nostril, then glanced in my direction. She looked past me, around me, through me—as if expecting anybody *but* me. I'd come to this party because I'd been sitting next to my roommate Jason in Green Library when she'd invited him. She and Jason had hooked up on the first day of orientation and were the dorm's first couple.

I shouldered my way through a knot of athletic-looking guys, all about a half-foot taller than me, to a makeshift bar laid out over Megan's sink. I fixed myself a Cape Cod, the only drink I'd learned to stomach in my first two weeks of college. The mirror started floating around the room like an *hors d'oeuvre* tray, from one pair of shaky hands to the next. When it got to me, I kept it going to my right, shielding it from a breeze coming through the open window.

The irony of all this lay in the fact that I grew up on Poco Way in the East Side of San Jose, a barrio where coke and heroin were as easy to buy as Diet Pepsi and cigarettes. Every intersection along McCreery had its *cholo* dealer in 48-inch dickies doling out baggies through open-windowed cruise-bys. My older brother Martín made his living slanging too, but after a freebasing explosion blew off two of his fingers and welded the others into a clump, he stopped bringing drugs into our house. He started doing all his work out of his partner Spider's place on Story and forbade him from talking business when I was around. Later, when he heard that my eighth-grade teacher had pronounced me her most gifted student, he swapped his bed in our room for the couch so I'd have a quiet place to study by myself.

He was on my ass all the time the way, I guess, my mother would have been if she hadn't been so wiped out every morning after a night of slogging a mop across a department store floor. He checked up on my grades and picked me up from school every day so I couldn't get jumped into the world of gangs and slangers that had been his second family since he was ten.

"Finally a Morales is going to climb out of this shit-hole of a neighborhood," he would say as he hustled breakfast together for me in the morning. "And when you buy a house in the hills, make sure it's a two-bedroom, 'cause I ain't sleeping on no fucking couch when I come and stay with you."

By the time I finished high school, I had a transcript spiked with A's. Getting into Stanford was just a matter of getting the application in on time and making sure to check the "Mexican-American" box under "Ethnic Background."

The mirror came back to Megan just as Jason came in. He was wearing shorts and a hooded sweatshirt. Dirty white socks had collapsed over his Stan Smiths, and his hair was matted to his forehead like he'd rushed over from tennis practice without showering. Megan threw him a wild smile and made room for him on her beanbag chair. She tapped out the rest of her vial and with her student ID arranged two pencil-thick lines. These she shaped into the letters JS, then handed him the straw. From across the room I tried to get his attention, but his face had already lit up like a siren. Megan laughed, put her hand on his knee.

I looked around for someone to start a conversation with, but no one seemed to notice me. Being only five-foot seven had worked to my advantage in the barrio—nobody noticed me, so nobody hassled me. But I was leaving all that behind me. I'd entered a place where you didn't have to watch your back every minute to survive, and I was going to stake my claim in it. For once I was going to stand out.

I went up to someone from Savannah I knew from my stats class. He was talking with a broad-shouldered guy with shoulder-length hair. "I know somebody who went to high school with her," Savannah was saying. "She only had a three-point-two. Nobody gets into this school with a three-point-two."

"Not unless Daddy's got his fingers on a few strings," the guy with the hair said.

"Four million dollars worth," drawled Savannah. "All tied around the balls of this institution's trustees."

"It'll catch up with her."

"Just like things are catching up with her Daddy," Savannah said. There was a low murmur of laughter. "What about you, Jorge?" he said to me. "Did your old man endow a path for you into this school with a hefty donation?"

"The only thing my dad ever put his money into was liquor," I said. "When he kicked off, I don't think he even had any functioning organs to donate."

This got a laugh out of them, but when I came back from refilling my drink, they'd moved to another side of the room.

I hung around long enough to finish off a couple more Cape Cods, then went back to my room to scour the part-time listings. I'd sucked enough scholarship money out of the school for tuition, but still needed cash for books and other expenses. Martín had said he'd send me a couple hundred each month, but I didn't want him taking on any extra drug work on my account.

In a few minutes Jason stumbled in, clutching his chest as if he were mid-cardiac. He kicked the door shut behind him, spun once on his heel, and collapsed face-up on his bed.

"I can't take this anymore," he said. "This Wall Street princess was supposed to be an easy score."

"Megan still not letting you past first base?" I said.

"I don't get it," he said. "Rumor is, she had a revolving bedroom door in high school."

"Maybe she's laying low now that her dad's in the spotlight."

"You might be able to soften her up for me," he said. "She's having trouble with econ, thinks she might need some help. I told her you A.P.'ed out of it and might be willing."

I shot him a look. "Little Miss Hoover keeps me up until three every night with her snow-fests, floats by me like I'm last Tuesday's leftovers, and now she wants my help?"

"She likes you well enough."

"She doesn't know my name. Keeps calling me 'George.' Face it, I don't register."

He threw a pillow at me. "Never mind. I'll get what I want soon enough. Then *bam*"— he slammed his fist into his palm— "She won't know what hit her."

He hopped to his feet and fed a tape into his tapedeck, started doing spastic air guitar to some Black Flag. I stuffed some books into my backpack, then headed out, stepping over a pile of Jason's *Hustlers* and *Penthouses*.

"Do something about these, will you? The last thing I need is to be labeled a pervert by association. Getting a date around here is hard enough as it is."

Passing through the courtyard I heard some Bob Seeger drifting down from Megan's second-story room. She was at her window, touching her string of pearls with her fingertips as she laughed with someone out of sight. I stopped to watch her. The first day I'd met her, she'd mistaken me for one of the movers that were bringing in her things that she'd had shipped across country. Since then I'd gritted my teeth every time she addressed me in her bland, arid tone. But from a distance it was hard not to look at her. She was like something out of a Hollywood movie—unreal, fabricated. Even her most ordinary gestures had a fake quality that seemed to come from coaching.

✿ ✿ ✿

That night I called Elena, my high school girlfriend from San Jose. She wasn't my girlfriend anymore, though. I'd convinced her that we should break up so we could see other people once I'd started school. But after just three weeks, I could tell my options were going to be limited. I was starting to think I'd made a mistake.

"Talk to me in Spanish," I said when she picked up.

"You know my Spanish is terrible," she said.

"I don't care," I said. "I just need to hear it."

"Poor Jorge," she said, switching languages. "Lost in the land of the *gringos*. Will he ever find his way home?"

"Back into your arms, you mean?"

She laughed that sweet, buttery laugh that had gotten my attention the first time I'd met her. I'd been standing in line at the cineplex to see Clint Eastwood's *Tightrope* and had looked over my shoulder to see a wiry, dark-eyed girl in stretch pants and halter top. She was there by herself, she said, because her girlfriends thought she was crazy to want to see a film with three killings in the first twenty minutes. She was the only girl I'd ever met whose appraisal of a movie went up with the amount of gunfire in it.

"It's good to hear your voice," I said. "When are you going to come up and see the campus?"

"I already saw it," she said. "Remember? Last July."

"All right. Then when are you going to come up and see me? Or have I already been replaced?"

"It was your idea to move on," she said.

"And you're a moving-on kind of girl," I said.

"That's right," she said. "But I don't think you have to worry about the competition just yet. I wants me an educated Mexy-Can."

We talked for nearly an hour before Jason came in. "Why don't you come up tomorrow?" I said. "We can catch that new Van Damme movie."

"Twice the blood and mayhem of his last one?" she said.

"Two big thumbs down from the fat *and* the skinny guy."

"You know all my weak spots," she said.

Oc Oc Oc

That night the manager at the campus Coffee House called wanting to know if I could start the job I'd applied for the next evening. I called Elena to cancel our date, told her I'd get back to her as soon as I knew my work schedule.

My first night on the job was five hours of mashing together tuna sandwiches and being splatter-scorched with hot espresso. When I finally got back to the room, Jason was lying on his bed with a sour look on his face. The stereo was blasting an old Ramones song. I turned it down.

"You look like you've been working knee-deep in shit," he said.

"You look like you've been eating it," I said.

"Figuratively, yes. I lost my first match today."

"Oh," I said. "It's just one match though, right?"

"Against some low-ranked geek I should have wiped across the court."

"You'll come back."

"I'd better," he said. "It's the only thing that got me into this school. Did you know I didn't lose—"

"A single match your senior year. I know, I know."

"Well, it's true," he said. "I think I need to go out and get fucked up."

"There's a party at Alpha Delts," I said.

"Get changed. Let's go."

"Can't. I've got prep shift in the morning."

"Deadbeat," he said, and flipped a pillow behind his head.

"Why don't you go with Megan?" I said. "Or have you given up on the ice princess?"

"Not even," he said. "Sex is a power game. I've got to let her think she's winning for a while before I get what I want."

❦ ❦ ❦

That night the thumping from Megan's room was even louder than usual. I counted down to zero from a hundred, then flung my covers off and threw on my robe. I knotted it and went out the door, tore down the hall, started pounding on her door. She answered in a T-shirt and running shorts. I had expected to see a swarm of partiers, but she was alone. A rubber dental massager dangled from the corner of her mouth.

"Don't you know some people have morning classes?" I shouted over the bass. The music was so loud I could see the glass trembling in the picture frames on her wall. "Not everybody's schedule starts at noon after lines and a cocktail."

She drew the hair away from her eyes with a hooked finger, yawned. "Sorry," she said. She put the massager down and spun the volume dial on her stereo. The room stopped shaking.

"The next time I'm calling the cops." I said. "You must be violating every noise ordinance from here to Topeka."

She pressed two fingers to her lips and squinted at me, as if I were a potted plant she was trying to find the right place for. Then she said, "As long as you're here, I wanted to ask you something."

I stared at her.

"Jason said you won't help me with Econ."

I pulled my robe closed. "Look," I said, "I'm loaded with twenty units and I have to work. You know, that thing that comes after you blow your trust fund."

A scent of lavender soap drifted off her body. "Oh well," she shrugged. "I thought I could do you a favor."

"Excuse me? Do *me* a favor?" Blood surged to my face.

She blinked at me. "I thought at fifty dollars an hour. . ."

"You want to pay me?"

"Jason said you were looking for extra money."

"The career center can set you up with a tutor."

"Not one that lives a hundred yards away," she said. "See, I was thinking this way I could get your help whenever I got stuck. You could keep track of hours and then bill me, the way lawyers do."

"Billable hours," I said.

"Four, five times a week?"

She pulled out an unfinished problem set from her desk drawer and handed it to me. I could see right away she'd started with the wrong formula. "All right," I said. "Pull up a chair. The clock's running."

We stayed up working until three. As I guided her through each problem, she crossed and uncrossed her legs, spun her rings, got up to change radio stations. With study habits like these, there was no question about it: Her father's endowment for a new chemistry building had paid her way in. She was going to need a whole army of tutors by the end of the semester.

She arrived the next day to our study session a half hour late, then an hour late to the next one, each time blinking dimly, as if she'd just gotten off a long, monotonous train ride.

"You're not taking this seriously," I said. "I thought you were in trouble in this class."

"I am," she said. "I just need a passing grade to fulfill a requirement." She shrugged, unwrapped a stick of gum. "Anyway, it's just one class."

Jason had told me that she wanted to go all the way through law school, but I couldn't believe she'd ever get those kinds of grades. Grades had gotten me out of the barrio, but I started to realize that for Megan they had no such value. Whatever her grades, her life would go on more or less smoothly, on a course that had been shaped by forces she'd probably never thought about.

A week later, as I waited in Meyer Library for her to show up late for the third time in a row, I decided we were wasting each other's time. I had my speech ready: *Let's forget about this. I don't care about the money. I'm not going to help you if you're not going to value my time.*

But instead, when she sat down across from me, I said, "Everyone is saying you've had tit implants. Is that true?" I glared at her, not daring to let my eyes drop below her neckline.

She stared at me for a moment. Then her face flashed alive with the first real smile she'd ever given me—broad, girlish, completely unrestrained.

"Well," she said, "if you must know, yes."

"Doesn't that seem vain? Doesn't that seem . . . stupid?"

"Why? If I have the resources to go through with it . . ."

"Just because you can afford to do something doesn't mean you should."

"We all take advantage of what's available to us. That's human nature."

"Not everybody's nature," I said. "Not mine."

"Yes, yours," she said. She shifted in her chair. "For instance, you took advantage of your ethnic background to get into this school, didn't you?"

"I had good grades in school. . ."

"But were they good enough to have gotten you in if you were white?"

"That's different. We're talking about compensating for past inequities. It's a matter of fairness."

"Fair to your race, maybe," she said. "But fair to the guy who busted his butt for a three-point-nine and couldn't get in because he was Irish? I don't think he'd look at it that way."

She gave me a smug smile, then opened her books. I opened mine, trying as hard as I could not to be attracted to her.

🙟 🙟 🙟

Megan came by my room the next morning in a fluster. Her hair was up in a scarf that was knotted under her chin, and she had on black cat-eye sunglasses. She looked like a '50s housewife escaping to do secret government spy work.

"Can you give me a ride?" she said. "I need to pick up something from a friend and I overslept."

"What's wrong with your car?" I said.

"Nothing. I overdid it last night at the boat house party, so I left my car there. I'll even pay you. Twenty bucks."

We went out to the lot and got into my beat-up GTO. I swung out onto Campus Drive, then followed her directions down Middlefield out to Los Altos. We turned left down a street of big, two-story houses with plush lawns and gardens. She told me to pull over in front of a gated Tudor mansion set far back behind its own forest of baby redwoods. She jumped out before I'd even stopped the car.

"Leave it running," she said.

I tuned the radio to K101. John Lennon's "Imagine" came on. He was just getting to the part about the world living as one, and I was thinking, *Yeah, right,* when Megan came trotting down the red stone path.

"You're a life-saver," she said, hopping into the car.

I pulled away from the curb, spun the car around. She started tucking sprays of hair under her scarf. She hummed along with Lennon. I pulled up to a traffic light. The engine's soft grumble filled the car.

"Aren't you worried?" I said.

"About what, Tutor?"

"Getting caught?"

She looked at me. "Do you want some?"

"No, thanks."

"Mind if I do?"

I shrugged. She took the vial out of her pocketbook, scooped out a small white mound with her dorm key.

The light turned green. I gunned the car forward.

"Are you mad?" she said. "I'm really sorry. I should have told you. It's just that I had to get here by ten."

"I'm not mad," I said, though my grip was pretty tight on the wheel. "I was just . . . wondering."

"About?"

I was thinking: *What in the world does Jason see in you?* But instead, I said, "What in the world do you see in Jason?"

She laughed. "I don't know. He's someone to be with."

"Doesn't sound very inspired."

"I've always had someone," she said. "Why should I be alone if I don't have to?"

"So you're not serious about him?"

"Why do you ask?"

"I just think you could do better."

"Like you, for instance?"

"Absolutely not," I said, throwing the car by mistake from fourth into second. We jerked forward.

"You dislike me that much?" she said.

"Look," I said, "I don't think you could ever understand where I come from. I was seeing neighbors getting shot when I was eight."

"We have more in common than you think. We both have things we want to leave behind."

"I can't imagine what that would be in your case."

"This mess with my father for one."

"And your reputation for another?"

She looked at me. "Don't hold back any punches," she said.

"Well, that's why you won't sleep with Jason, isn't it?"

She folded her arms, looked out the window. "Let's just say having someone write 'class slut' across your yearbook picture in black marker is good incentive for reevaluation."

✿ ✿ ✿

The following week Jason flubbed two more matches against mid-ranked players from around the state. On Friday, he asked me and Megan to be in the stands to watch him play USC. Knowing we were there, he said, would make him play better.

I called Elena that day and asked her if she wanted to see a Stanford match. She drove up that weekend and met me at the dorm, and from there we walked over to varsity courts. It felt good to hold her hand again. I didn't bring up the subject of where our relationship stood. I wanted to pretend for a while that things were like they had always been between us.

The first game was underway when we got to the courts, Jason squaring off against a guy with long hair and a Zen-like expression. I held Elena's hand and looked around the stands for Megan, but didn't see her anywhere. I gave Elena a kiss every time Jason scored a point. I gave her a kiss every time he lost one.

He won the first three games 40-love, 40-30, 40-15, but then started having trouble with his serve. He double-faulted twice, then lost the next point with a sloppy backhand return. Then he smashed an easy lob past his opponent's baseline. Even from where we sat we could see his face darkening with each mistake, his jaw muscles bulging. The rest of the match was downhill, and it didn't take long for him to lose the match. A number of times he looked up into the stands. I gave him a thumbs-up sign, but he wasn't looking at me. I think he was looking for Megan.

Elena and I waited outside the gym for him afterwards. When he showed up, he had showered and changed.

"Tough competition," I said.

"Where was Megan?" he said.

"I don't know," I said. "Jason, this is Elena. Elena, Jason."

"I should have taken this guy," he said. "I knew all his flaws."

"I thought you played great anyway," Elena said. "I enjoyed watching."

Jason glared, not at her, but over her shoulder, as if she weren't there at all.

"Are you coming back to the dorm?" he said to me.

"Elena and I are going to dinner. Want to join us?"

"Never mind," he muttered, turning away.

"Nice people you're meeting here," Elena said when he was gone.

"He's carrying some really high expectations," I said. "The coaches are saying he could be the next McEnroe."

"Oh. That makes everything different."

"Look," I said. "You don't know what it's like to be under that kind of pressure. I'm feeling it too. Everyone here is."

"No," she said, "I've never been under any pressure."

"You know what I mean," I said.

"Yes," she said, crossing her arms tensely. "I know what you mean."

*Ω̃c *Ω̃c *Ω̃c

Megan called the next morning and said she'd pay me twenty bucks to drive her to Los Altos again. Someone had keyed her car and it was going to be in the shop for a few days. I went by around noon and was about to knock when I heard shouting from her room. Her door flew open and Jason stormed out past me. His fists and jaw were clenched, his face fluorescing with rage. I watched him beat his way down the hall and out of sight. Then I peered into Megan's room.

She was leaning against her desk, her face covered with two trembling hands as she sobbed. Across the floor a ceramic desk lamp lay shattered in pieces along with books and broken picture frames. And against the wall, her laptop computer lay in a heap where it had been thrown.

She pulled the hair out of her face when she saw me. "Welcome to the scene of a couple's first fight," she said.

"Obviously a big one," I said. "Should I come back?"

She waved me in. "I don't get it," she said after a moment. "I don't know what's gotten into him."

"He's been weird since his losing streak started," I said.

"Which is all my fault, according to him."

"Meaning?"

"I forgot about his match yesterday. He says he was so worried about me he couldn't concentrate. Oh, and let's see. I'm a sex tease, and that's why he's been losing his matches."

"That's some logic," I said.

"He should consider law school," she said.

"He's not used to losing. Did you know in high school. . ."

"He didn't lose a match his senior year?"

We both laughed.

"I came by to give you that ride," I said. "You ready?"

"Oh shit," she said, covering her mouth. "I forgot to call you. My source called this morning. He couldn't get me any this time. The police are starting some kind of crack-down. The whole peninsula is closing shop until it's over." She bit her cuticle, looked out the window.

"Well, it's not like you need it, is it?" I said.

"I'm not addicted, if that's what you mean. Some other people were depending on me for Monte Carlo night, that's all."

"They can't go without?"

"You're right. God, listen to how I must sound. What do you say we get off this stupid campus? Go out to San Gregorio? It's still warm enough for the beach."

"Don't you want to patch things up with Jason?"

"That can wait," she said. "Anyway, at least with you I only have to worry about sarcasm getting thrown around."

Cc Cc Cc

That night, when I was finally alone, I called my brother Martín. "Yes," I said, "I'm definitely coming home for Mom's birthday. But listen, I'm calling about something else. It's something I want to keep just between you and me, okay?" I switched the phone to my other ear. "I have a little favor I want you to do for me. You're not going to like it, but I really need this from you."

Cc Cc Cc

When I got home that Saturday, my mother came running down the hall of our floor of the housing project I grew up in to greet me. Her eyes were full of tears, her face trembling with excitement. Martín was right behind her, trying to look casual, but he was excited too. I could tell by the way he kept patting himself on the chest, like an old woman trying to keep from fainting.

That afternoon he did most of the cooking while I caught up with my mother in the living room. I told her about classes, about how the campus was so enormous that I still got lost sometimes and had to ask for directions. "You've never seen so much open space," I said. "Everything looks like a country club on *Dynasty*. You could fit a dozen projects into the main part of the campus alone." In the kitchen, Martín listened, coming to the door with a knife or mixing bowl in his hand every few minutes to ask questions. The more I told them—about classes, about Megan and Jason, about the wealth I saw every day—the more curiously they looked at me and shook their heads, as if I'd drifted away to some other world and had come back someone they didn't quite recognize.

The house began to fill with the smells that until then I had taken for granted: the sweet cornmeal for tamales, bitter chocolate for the *atole,* acrid roasting *chiles,* buttery pie crusts baking in the oven. I used to complain that we never had pot roast or meatloaf the way most people did, but this time I was glad for what I used to call the same old thing.

That night, after my mother had gone to bed, I came into the living room where Martín was sitting on the couch. "Still having trouble sleeping?" I said. My brother was a long-time insomniac, had never been able to get to sleep before three in the morning. He used to wander the streets at night when I was a kid, which is how he got into drugs.

He was watching *The French Connection* on TV. I sat down next to him.

"I've seen this one," I said. "Best chase sequence in any movie you'll ever see."

He kept watching the TV. His face flickered with the movie's changing scenes. "I got what you wanted," he said. "I don't know why I did it. You know I've always tried to keep you away from this stuff."

"I told you, it's not for me."

"I don't like the idea."

"This stuff is all over the place up there."

"You're not going to do it yourself?"

"You know I have no interest in it."

"Man, if I ever find out . . ."

"Martín, you have my word. It's not like I didn't grow up with it all around me."

"You swear it's just this once?"

"I swear."

I followed him into the bright light of the kitchen. He sat down at the table and reached into his jacket, brought out three inch-wide ziplocks filled with white powder.

"Thanks," I said. "You don't know what a big favor you're doing me."

He put his mangled hand on the table, which was what he always did when he wanted to warn me about not making the same mistakes he had. He stared at it for a long time. I was expecting some kind of lecture. But instead, he said, "You have a girlfriend up there yet?"

"No," I said.

"There's no one you like?" he said.

"Just Elena," I said. "But she's here, I'm there . . ."

He thought for a long time, still staring at his hand. "You should have a girlfriend," he said finally. "Don't wait too long. Get yourself a girlfriend."

✿✿ ✿✿ ✿✿

Megan took a taste out of the plastic bag. "Oh, good stuff," she said. She kissed me on the cheek, then jumped over to her dresser and pulled out a wad of twenties. "Ellen and Iris are going to die when I tell them."

"You seem better," I said. "Things all straightened out between you and Jason?"

"He apologized for his tantrum," she said. She gestured to a vase of roses on her desk.

I left her making phone calls, then went out to my Chemistry class. When I got back, I had a message from someone named Diane Schwartz, a friend of Megan's who wanted me to call her back as soon as possible. I did.

"Thanks for calling," she said when she picked up. "Megan said you had some Cola. Do you think you could get me some?"

There were two more messages—both from friends of Megan. I speed-dialed her room. "What the hell are you telling people?" I said. "I've got every Tom, Dick, and Junky calling me for coke."

"Sorry, Tutor," she said. "I guess I let it slip that it was you that got it for me. It won't happen again." Her voice was timbreless, nasal like she'd been crying.

"What's wrong?" I said.

"I think you jinxed me by mentioning Jason," she said.

"Not again," I said.

"Wanted me to give him a ride to practice, but I was too busy."

"You all right?"

"A little shaken. Honestly, Jorge. I'm not sure how much more of this I can take."

That afternoon I sat in the last row of the lecture hall during Western Civ. A guest lecturer droned on about Thomas Aquinas. I doodled in the columns of my notebook. I flipped over my syllabus and just for fun worked out how much I'd make if I were to get Megan's friends what they wanted. I could see how easily Martín had fallen into dealing—the perfect job for someone who was always up half the night.

I wasn't very serious about it, but I did need to start thinking about how I was going to make money. The Coffee House job was wearing me out, and I was only tutoring Megan once a week now. I stopped by Career Planning and Placement to look over the new listings.

Later that week, Megan called asking if there was any way I could get her friends more of the stuff I'd gotten her. "You could make a killing," she said, a little sing-song in her voice. "All other sources are dry. They'll pay whatever you ask."

"I don't know," I said. "It might be hard getting the stuff a second time."

I thought about it for a while. I figured it couldn't hurt to give Martín a try again. The worst that could happen was that he'd chew me out. In any case, I'd promised to come by sometime to help him repaint the living room. I drove down that weekend. Shifting over a lane to get off at my exit, I remembered his partner Spider.

I got off two exits past the projects and swung west of the freeway to Spider's neighborhood. Until Martín's accident I used to ride with Martín to and from this neighborhood when he'd make his pick-ups. Having a kid in the car made everything look normal, he used to say. I hadn't seen Spider in a couple of years, but he was always nice to me on the phone when he'd call for my brother, and used to send me cards on holidays—even sent me five hundred dollars when I graduated from high school. I pulled up behind Spider's Chevy pickup in his driveway.

He recognized me right away when he opened the door, gave me a hug. "How's it going, *Tío*?" I said, which was what he used to like me to call him. I was ten before I figured out he wasn't really my uncle.

"Not bad, Moralito," he said. "If you're looking for your brother, he ain't here. Man, ain't you supposed to be in that fancy college or something?"

"I'm giving myself a little *vacación*," I said, letting my voice drop to the friendly street lilt that told people you were *firme*—cool, trustworthy. I said, "I got a little favor to ask you, Spide," and gave a friendly jab at the tarantula tattooed on his shoulder.

In his apartment his stereo display flashed to the music, which was coming out of enormous speakers mounted in the walls. He lowered the volume with a remote, then settled back into his couch. He pushed aside an ashtray heaped with butts and put his feet up. "What can I do for you, Moralito?"

"First of all, nothing about this to Martín," I said. "Otherwise, I'm out of here like a ghost and you ain't never seen me."

A grin crept across his face. "Name your candy," he said.

"How much coke can I get for this?" I threw some money on the table.

He motioned for me to follow him to the bedroom. The walls were hung with fluorescent posters of jaguars and pythons that glowed under a black light. He untacked one of the posters and opened a safe mounted into the wall. From it he took out a black wooden box with gold hinges. It was filled with plastic vitamin bags, all full of cocaine.

"You want to weigh the stuff out?" he said.

"I trust you."

After we had talked a little longer, he walked me out to my car. "You've got that whole campus of rich kids to sell to," he said. "You just let me know how I can help. I think we could work really well together."

He followed me out to the driver's side of my car, leaned his head through the open window. "Keep it around sixty on your way back," he said. "There's nothing more suspicious to the cops than a muscle car doing the limit."

Back on campus, I drove around in the twilight delivering to Megan's friends, then headed out to the Stanford shopping center to buy a blazer for Monte Carlo night, the fall dorm fundraiser. I browsed the racks at Macy's, not sure what I was looking for. I'd never owned even semi-formal clothes before. I pulled a blue jacket with gold buttons. The soft, lightweight wool settled against my skin like a sigh. I'd never felt anything so elegant.

"We'll need to take up the sleeves," said a salesman appearing in the mirror I was in front of. "But other than that, it's a good fit."

I bought it with cash, then wandered through the rest of the upscale mall, thinking about what else I could buy if I wanted to. I'd never carried that much money before, and kept feeling my back pocket to make sure my wallet hadn't been lifted. I bought sunglasses at Nordstrom's—a pair so dark I couldn't see my own eyes in my reflection—then a new shirt and a watch I'd admired. I left the mall with my heart pounding. I'd just spent more money in an hour than I normally did in a month, and I still had money left. I thought about going back to buy something for Megan, but thought Jason might misinterpret it.

Back at the dorm, Jason was just coming in from the showers. He started combing his hair at the mirror with a seriousness I'd never seen before, adjusting each blonde curl on his forehead.

"Something special tonight?" I said.

"You could say that," he said. "Megan asked me to come by her room tonight. Her roommate is out of town for the weekend. I think she's finally ready. Tonight's going to be the night."

"Good luck," I said. "I won't wait up."

"Luck's not going to have anything to do with it," he said.

*Ϙ *Ϙ *Ϙ

Elena came up a little later for dinner and a movie. I hadn't called her in a while and wanted to make things up to her for the last time we'd been together. I wore some of the new clothes I'd bought. For some reason I expected her to comment on them, but she didn't. The Van Damme movie I'd planned to take her to at the Guild wasn't playing anymore when we got there. Instead, they were showing the '70s remake of *The Great Gatsby* with Robert Redford. But the film kept jamming in the projection booth, so we never saw how it ended. That was fine with me, because it was one of the most boring movies I'd ever seen.

We walked the downtown strip.afterwards, then went back to the dorm. Jason was there, doing lay-up shots of crumpled paper into a waste basket propped up on his stereo speakers.

"Why aren't you with Megan?" I said.

"She forgot she had a thing to go to," he said. "She cancelled on me."

"A *thing?*"

"Committee meeting. Something about planning Monte Carlo night. She won't be done until after midnight."

"Jason, you remember Elena."

"Yeah, hi. How are you?" He kept doing lay-up shots. I glared at him.

He stopped. "Like I was saying," he muttered. "On my way out."

Elena and I stood watching him grumpily put on his shoes and grab his coat.

When he was gone, I watched Elena's hips shift under her skirt like a bell as she went over to the window. The copper light of the courtyard lamps outside cast a delicate glow over her dark shoulders. She'd gone out of her way to look good tonight, and I should have been more attracted to her than ever, but I wasn't.

She strolled over from the window, arms folded. "You seem so serious," she said.

"College does that," I said.

"You've always overworked yourself." She sat next to me on the bed, glided her fingers through my hair. "It's funny how fast people change," she said.

"Do I seem different?"

"A little sadder, somehow."

"I guess I'm always a little tired these days."

She leaned towards me and kissed me, gently at first, lips barely touching as if waiting for a spark to jump between us. I put my hand on her waist, glided it up her torso. I kissed harder, the way I used to. Maybe she felt as little as I did, because she smiled at me and let one of those sighs that says an evening has come to its end.

"Well," she said, drawing away gracefully, "Thanks for finding the time in your busy schedule."

"It was great to see you again. I'd ask you to stay, but. . ."

"Your roommate."

"Right."

"We'll talk?"

"Soon."

"Keep an eye out for that new Eastwood movie," she said.

I kissed her goodbye. When she was gone, I went to the window and watched her reappear in the courtyard below. I kept expecting her to look back over her shoulder, to wave one last time, the way people always did in the movies. But she just kept walking.

I leaned back on my elbows and let the last few minutes play over in my mind. The clock said just past nine, too early to go to bed. I pulled on my coat to go out for a walk.

On my way out through the courtyard, through half averted blinds, I made out the silhouette of Megan in her room, talking on her phone and pacing excitedly.

❧ ❧ ❧

A few days before Monte Carlo night, calls started coming in from people wanting last-minute weekend party favors. "I don't know," I began each conversation when I called back. "It's pretty late notice. I might have to charge extra for the rush."

I had given up my job at the Coffee House the week before and had decided not to look for something new until next quarter. I decided to take a few more orders to get me through the quarter. I put on my sunglasses and headed south to make another pick up from Spider.

The day of the Monte Carlo party, I went around campus making drop-offs. I kept my sunglasses on and my expression stony. "I had to go through a lot of trouble to get this," I told each customer flatly. "Next time I hope you'll do me the courtesy of a little advance notice."

Back at the dorm, people in coats and ties and formal dresses were already drifting towards the dining hall for Monte Carlo night. I found Jason struggling with his tie in our room. After a quick shower I slipped into my new clothes. I ran a comb through my hair at the sink.

"Let's get going," he said.

"You can't hurry perfection," I said.

"Especially when it's out of your reach," he said.

"Go fuck yourself," I said. "But hand me that tie first."

He wadded it up and threw it at me. "Are you the same person I moved in with?"

"I'm not taking shit from anybody anymore."

When I was ready, we headed towards the dining hall. "Aren't we stopping for Megan?" I said as we passed her door.

"We'll meet her there. Come on, I want to get there before some prig R.A. decides to read up on university liquor policy."

The dining hall had been cleared to make room for blackjack, craps, baccarat, roulette and poker tables. And prize booths, where chips could be turned in for prizes instead of cash. At the exchange booth I bought ten dollars in chips, then traded some of them in for a Manhattan. In a few minutes I was feeling loose in the shoulders. A music theory major from Toyon I'd sold to thumped me lightly on the shoulder.

"You saved the weekend, Morales," he said.

"He saved our asses," someone else said.

"Let's drink to Morales."

"Morales is the man."

"The wizard," someone said.

"The king."

I raised my glass. "Just a small service in the name of school spirit," I said. As I made my way around the room, I heard, "Thanks, Morales" and "Good work, Morales." I jangled the chips in my pocket, went from table to table putting down bets.

I saw Megan walk in then. Several people standing next to me at craps looked up. She was wearing a white strapless dress that billowed out like a tulip below her hips, but clung to every curve above her waist. Other girls were wearing white too, but hers was the whitest thing in the place. Diamond studs caught the light, shattered it. Everyone stared. Although she looked more beautiful than I had ever seen her, she also looked cold in that dress. Even from a distance I could see that she was shivering. She pulled a thin, transparent silvery-threaded shawl close around her shoulders.

I found Jason at blackjack, glumly taking up a hand he'd just been dealt.

"Megan's here," I said.

He peeled up his cards, scraped the felt for the dealer to hit.

"She's over by the water cooler," I said. "I don't think I've ever seen her look so good."

"I see her," he said, but he didn't look up. The dealer pushed him over twenty-one. He tossed the cards, put down another stack of chips.

"Mind telling me what's going on?"

"We're not going out anymore," he said. "That's all."

"The roommate's always the last to know," I said.

"Happened a few days ago. I didn't say anything because . . . well, I just didn't, I don't know why."

He folded his next hand, then turned and leaned against the table with his back to her. "Let's get out of here," he said. "I hate these phony events. Monte Carlo. Give me a break."

We walked through the lounge and out into the courtyard. He leaned against one of the bike racks outside the front steps. I took off my blazer, let the night breeze wick away the mild sweat that the warm dining hall lights had produced.

"Has she said anything to you?" he said.

"No. This is a total surprise to me. Want to talk about it?"

"No. Not really."

He looked at the ground, sucked in his lower lip. I tried to think of something to say, but the fact was, I'd been having a great time and wanted to go back inside.

"I need to walk," he said. "I need to get away from this place."

"You do that," I said, and patted his elbow. I turned to go.

"Jorge," he said.

I stopped. "Yeah?"

"Let me know if Megan says anything." He didn't look up. "Or if you notice anything about her."

"Like?"

"Just anything . . . that seems . . . different."

"Sure," I said. I swung my blazer over my shoulder. "Be easy on yourself, okay?"

Inside I noticed I was starting to sober up and I didn't like the feeling. I had a couple vodkas straight up. But I didn't go over to talk to Megan. It was a lot more enjoyable watching her from a distance, watching other people watching her. A sad expression on her face made her look older, added a new depth to her beauty. Several times I saw her break away from a conversation and walk out to the restroom, then come back with an easy smile on her face that would last just a few minutes. Then the sadness would fall over her features again, and she would once more be off to the restroom.

I watched her for a long time without going over to talk to her.

❧❧ ❧❧ ❧❧

When I went by her room the next day, her roommate Doreen told me she'd gone home to New York. "She said not to tell anyone anything," she said, crossing her arms.

As I turned away she said, "You're Jason's roommate, aren't you?"

I told her I was.

"That's what I thought," she said, her upper lip crimping into a scowl.

I left a message for Megan, asking her to call me as soon as she got back. I week went by and I heard nothing from her. I checked the papers every morning, looking for news about her father. I figured there'd been a turn in his trial, but I saw nothing. Then, coming out of Tressider Store one day, I saw her stirring a cup of coffee at one of the picnic tables outside the Coffee House.

"How long have you been back?" I said, coming up behind her.

She looked over her shoulder "Hi, Jorge. How are you?"

"Why didn't you call?" I said.

"I'm sorry," she said. "There's so much going on right now."

"Too much for you to return messages?"

"Things are crazy."

"Is it your dad?"

"Not exactly. Personal stuff."

"Personal stuff. Oh. Okay. Well, that explains everything, in a *Cliffs Notes* kind of way."

"Wait a minute," she said. "Let me give you a ride back to the dorm."

We found her car parked illegally at the bollards outside the Union. I got in and she pulled out onto Campus Drive. Usually she drove carelessly, cutting people off, drifting into lanes without signaling. But today her driving was sharp, attentive, quick.

"I can't explain everything that's going on right now," she said. "I wish I could, but I just can't."

"Because you don't trust me?" I said.

"Nothing like that."

"Look," I said, "Jason told me you guys broke up. You might have at least mentioned it."

"What else did Jason tell you?"

"What am I, Liz Smith?"

"You're right. That's not a fair question. You're his roommate." She drew the hair away from her face. "I really am sorry," she said, her voice cracking.

She tried to turn her head then, but I already could see tears coming to her eyes.

"So what's really going on?" I said.

"In a few days I'll be able to explain everything. Right now you're just going to have to. . ."

"Never mind," I said. "Drop me off at the next corner. I feel like walking all of a sudden."

She pulled over at Bowdoin. "You and Jason shouldn't have broken up," I said. "The two of you deserved each other." I got out and slammed the door.

❧ ❧ ❧

Spider called later that week, wanting to know when I was going to place my next order. I froze where I was standing at the window the moment I recognized his voice. I'd never given him my number and had made sure it was unlisted with the university. I had no idea how he'd tracked me down.

"I haven't had any requests recently," I told him.

"Don't tell me you can't use the money," he said. "Life must be expensive up there in that rich place."

"Really, I'm doing fine."

"No girlfriend you want to buy something for? Someone you want to impress?"

"Nothing's going on right now," I said. "Maybe in a couple. . ."

"Come on, man. You have that whole big fucking campus and you're telling me you can't find a couple of people who need a little help staying up at night?"

"Listen," I said. "You've been a big help to me. I appreciate that. But I never said I wanted to be one of your regulars."

He laughed. "You're already a regular."

Static crackled between us for a few seconds. Then I said, "I'll call you in a couple of weeks before finals."

"Great," he said. "Your brother's coming over later. I'll be sure to tell him you're doing okay."

"Don't say anything to him."

"Just give your *tío* a call when you're ready."

I hung up. *Tío.* I shivered at the word.

I tried to go back to studying, but Spider's voice kept going through my head. I decided to take a walk to clear my thoughts. Just then the door banged open, sending papers flying off Jason's desk. Jason staggered in, his face scorched pink by wind, sweaty curls pasted to his forehead. His T-shirt ws soaked through like he'd just ran a marathon.

"Where the hell have you been?" he rasped. "I've been looking all over for you. What am I going to do? What the fuck am I going to do?"

"The *Reader's Digest* version, please," I said. "I've got work to do."

He sat down on his bed, ran iron-tense fingers through his hair. I could see the tendons straining out.

"She's done it," he said. "She's really gone and done it."

"Help me out here," I said. "One word or two? First word sounds like . . .?"

"Rape," he said. Then, in a voice I could barely hear, "The bitch is accusing me of rape."

He lowered himself to the edge of his bed. "You've got to help me. You know Megan as well as anyone. You've got to talk to her."

"What did you do to her?" I said.

"Nothing," he said.

"She wouldn't make up something like this."

"I was just playing around with her." His voice climbed to a squeal. "She was all coked up. She got confused or paranoid or something. She totally overreacted." He dropped his face into his hands. His shoulders started to quake.

I stared at him. Then all at once he stood up and grabbed a book off his desk and gave it a violent Frisbee-hurl at the window. It hit the blinds and they came down in a crash over his desk, scattering pencils everywhere.

"The *bitch*," he screamed. He pounded his fist against the bedframe. "She was asking for it."

❧ ❧ ❧

When I went by Megan's, Doreen was sweeping out the room. All of Megan's things were gone, her side of the room bare except for wastebaskets overflowing with discarded things.

"She's moved off campus until after the hearing," Doreen said. "Nobody's supposed to know where she is."

"The hearing?"

"She's throwing the book at him. The case against her dad was dismissed. Now his lawyers have a whole new project to work on."

I tried not to think about it for the rest of the day. I didn't want to draw any conclusions until I'd heard from Megan. Then, leaving the dorm to take a stats exam, I saw a young red-headed woman waving at me from across the courtyard. I didn't recognize her, but I waved back, shielding my eyes. She ran across the grass quadrangle.

"Pretty awful what's happening with your roommate," she said, huffing.

"You could say that." I still didn't recognize her.

"How long were he and Megan going out?"

"And your name is?" I said.

"I'm with the *Daily*," she said. "I'm doing an article on the accusation."

"Terrific," I said. I put my sunglasses on, started walking again.

"Are you and Jason good friends?" She had a small microphone in her hand. It was connected to a recorder sticking out of her shirt pocket.

"What was your reaction when you heard the accusation?" she said.

I walked faster.

"Did Jason ever do anything that led you to think he was capable. . ."

I ripped the microphone out of her hand. The recorder popped out of her pocket, bounced a couple of times across the path. I gave it a kick across the lawn.

"Get the hell away from me," I said. I turned back to the dorm.

I felt all my energy drain out of me, leaving me feeling sick and hollow. In my room I dumped all my books in the corner and threw myself on the my bed. I was missing an important exam, but I couldn't bring myself to get up. Something inside me felt twisted out of place. I lay there for a long time, waiting for the feeling to go away.

❧ ❧ ❧

The next morning the phone calls started. Reporters from the *Chronicle*, the *Mercury-News*, even the local TV stations, all wanting any information I could give them about the world's most notorious Wall Street family. I took the phone off the hook, but couldn't concentrate, knowing that Megan might call. I reconnected it and called Elena.

"Everything's falling apart," I said. "I just slept through a test, and I can't concentrate for more than five minutes with this rape thing going on."

She talked to me for a few minutes, tried to calm me down. But I could tell from the agitation in her voice that she was in a hurry to get off the phone. Then someone in the background called out her name, a male voice I didn't recognize.

There was a pause in the conversation, but I didn't ask her who it was. I thanked her for listening and got off the line quickly. I gathered my things and headed out to the library.

That was when I saw the posters.

The first ones I saw were red-letter-size sheets of paper completely covering the kiosk outside the Union. Each one showed a blown-up photo of Jason taken from our freshman orientation book. Across the top it read "RAPIST." And across the bottom: "Date this man AT YOUR OWN RISK." As I continued to walk, I saw them everywhere—on every bulletin board and kiosk across campus, some even plastered to the sides of buildings. People everywhere were stopping to look at them. Then at the library, I noticed two people in the plush reading chairs staring at me and whispering. I was the rapist's roommate. I had to get off campus.

I drove out to the mall. The moment I got off campus, a breeze swept through my car's open windows. I wandered around for a while, looking into store windows, browsing through high-tech gadgets at the Sharper Image. Even though I was low on money, I bought a couple of new shirts. For a short while, I was able to forget.

That night the only thing I could concentrate on was processing the orders for coke that people wanted for the upcoming post-midterm parties. I was walking over to Sigma Chi to discuss the largest order their president had ever placed when Jason came running down the bike path to catch up with me. He seemed loose and lanky in a way that I hadn't seen in weeks, all the tension released from his frame.

"I'm free," he said. "Megan's dropped everything."

"How? What happened?"

"She went into a drug treatment program a couple of days ago. Nobody's going to take a cokehead seriously." He laughed, put his arm across my neck. "I have you to thank, Jorge. If you hadn't kept her supplied, she wouldn't have gone off the deep end."

I felt something in me buckle.

"What do you say we celebrate? Let's skip our classes and go out and get blasted."

My fist struck out. An electric pain shot through my arm. I'd hardly realized what I'd done before I saw Jason laying curled on his side on the bike path, a thin line of blood drizzling from his nose.

❧❧ ❧❧ ❧❧

I had to wait until Saturday to see Megan. Saturday was the clinic's only day for visitors. For some reason, I wasn't looking forward to seeing her, though I kept telling myself I was. I waited for her in the lounge area. When she appeared, she looked thinner, her skin shimmering with a translucence that made her look too fragile to hug. Weak fluorescent lighting further sucked the depth and color out of her.

"Tutor," she said.

I set some peonies I'd brought for her on the end table, but she didn't take her eyes away from me. She smiled, smoothed the cushion next to where I was sitting before she sat down. Her eyes sparkled with moisture.

"I'm so sorry," she said.

"I should have given you more slack," I said. "I should have known there was a reason you couldn't tell me."

"Are things okay with you?"

"They're kind of a mess. My grades are slipping. Jason and I aren't talking. It's a second Ice Age."

"Is everyone talking?"

I nodded. "Most people believe you, though."

"Do you believe me?" she said.

I took her hand, played with the silver rings on her fingers. "I've been trying not to think about it. I practically get sick when I do. This whole date-rape thing. . ."

"Is that what Jason told you it was? Date rape?"

"Wasn't it?"

She took a tissue from the front pocket of her checkered men's shirt, squeezed it into a ball. "I asked him to come by my room a couple of weeks ago. I was planning to break up with him. I just couldn't stand our fighting, him always blaming me for things. He had a different idea—thought I had invited him over to spend the night. I tried to tell him it wasn't working. He started getting mad."

"And then he. . ."

"No, not right away." She wiped her nose. "I was able to calm him down. He asked if he could stay and talk, clear things up. Said he wanted us to still be friends. I was surprised how well he was taking it. We had a couple drinks, started laughing about times we'd had. I was a little edgy from some coke I'd done earlier, so he offered me a couple of valium. All the time he kept pouring drinks. Finally I must have passed out. When I came to, he was on top of me . . ."

"Oh God," I said, and pulled her towards me. Her head went limp on my shoulder. "You could have come to me. You know that, don't you?"

"I wanted to talk to you more than anyone. But the lawyers, they said not to talk to anyone who knew Jason. Anyway, I never thought you liked me that much."

"I've always liked you," I said.

"Not at first," she laughed. "You thought I was terrible. God, Jorge, I miss those times. I even miss arguing with you."

Her words went through me, sword-like. "This shouldn't have happened to you," I said.

"Who could have known?"

"I did," I said. "I could have stopped it."

I realized then the reason for all my misery of the last few weeks. I had known all along that Jason would hurt her. I hadn't known, perhaps, that it would be a rape. But I had known something bad would happen. But the distance between Megan and me—that great, immeasurable distance between her world and mine—had allowed me to do nothing. Now I saw that distance for what it was: artificial and completely of my own making.

I held her for a long time, wanting her warmth to pass through me, penetrate to the center of my chilled heart. It was a long time before I could look at her. The white walls of the room seemed to lean in on us, compressing her pain into mine, making me feel more than ever the closeness I'd been denying. And with it, the burden of my responsibility to her.

"Forgive me," I said. "Please forgive me."

✿ ✿ ✿

That night there were two more messages from Spider wanting to know when I was going to pick up the order I'd left with him. It made me sick to hear his low, raspy voice. I opened the window to the cold, clear night and stood staring out into the courtyard. I wanted to cancel everything, but I had already taken money from dozens of people that were going to be furious if I pulled out. This would have to be my last killing, enough to set me up for the rest of the year. Then I wanted out for good.

It was an unexpectedly clear and humid night for December, washed clean by a recent Pacific storm, when I drove south to get the stuff. The air smelled sweet as I walked up Spider's front steps.

He was a little irritated by all the small bills, but smiled when he saw that it was all there. He tossed me a brown paper package. The weight of it as I hefted it took my breath away. I put it in my backpack and headed out to my car.

I shot back up 280 to avoid an accident the radio was reporting on 101. I leaned into my horn as a fancy two-toned BMW tried to wedge its way in front of me. I flashed my brights, pressed forward, hit the horn again.

Take it easy, I told myself. Calm down, I told myself. *Cálmate, cálmate.*

I rolled down my window, tugged at the front of my T-shirt.

Back on campus I rolled into the dorm lot, then got the backpack out of the trunk. I ran up the front steps and down the hall towards my room, humming a Human League song I'd just heard on the radio. I put my key in the door. It was unlocked.

The anger in my brother's face when I walked in sucked all the life out of me. He was sitting at my desk, his back to the window, outlined by the dark courtyard behind him.

"Martín," I said. "So you've decided to see what college life is all about."

I tried to smile, but only felt a weak twitching of my face muscles. I saw the fingers of his good hand curl over the side of the armrest, the veins bulging to the surface.

"What's that matter?" I said. "Your insomnia acting up again? How did you know I'd be up this late? Did Jason let you in?"

"Why did you do it?" he said.

"What do you mean?"

"Spider told me."

"It isn't what you think."

"Where is it?"

"I don't have it," I said, but I saw his eyes go to the backpack dangling at my knee. "Listen, Martín, I don't know what Spider told you . . ."

"It's over," he said. "You're getting out of this shitty business and so am I. Is that it?" He pointed to my backpack. He came towards me, put out his hand.

"Please, Martín." I backed up as he reached for it. He slammed me against the door, pinned me with his good arm. I twisted to get away, but he was too strong. The backpack slipped out of my grasp. "Martín, let's talk about this."

I followed him out into the hall. He turned left, then pushed through the doors to the men's shower room. Someone standing at the urinal looked over his shoulder at us. Martín walked past the toilets toward the tiled shower area, started unzipping the backpack.

"Martín, I've never actually done any of it."

He tore through the brown wrapper, dug his fingers into the plastic layer beneath. I grabbed at it, but he held it over his head. A burst of white powder showered down on our clothes, our hair, scattered across the tiles. Martín spun the shower knob to full force. I gasped, inhaled cold water. I tasted the sweet cocaine in my mouth for the first time. I backed away, choking. He shook out the rest of it, tossed the wrapping to the floor.

I leaned against the tiles, let the water rinse the white mess off my clothes. He turned the shower down. The trickle echoed.

Martín wiped the white muck off his arms. He sloshed at the water.

"You don't know what you've done," I said.

"I know," he said. "I know."

After a few minutes, he held out his good hand. I stared at it. My head was going numb from the cocaine, my heart racing.

Finally I took his hand. He yanked me towards him in one violent, angry jerk that nearly made my shoulder come out of its socket. He held me then, not the way a brother holds a brother, but the way a father holds a child nearly lost to drowning.

🙦 🙦 🙦

For the next two hours I lay in bed, trembling and sweating as I came down from the drug. Martín stayed with me, wiping my face with a cloth every few minutes.

"Don't worry," he said. "The sweat means it's almost over. You'll be able to fall asleep soon."

"I want to get out of here," I said. "I want to go home."

"You can't," he said. "Remember the plan. The house in the hills."

"Why do you want to live in the hills, anyway?" I said. "Why do you always say that?"

"Because I want a view of where we came from," he said. "I want to be able to see it without having to go back."

🙦 🙦 🙦

When Megan found out about the trouble I was in, she lent me the money to pay back everyone I'd taken cash from so I could concentrate on finishing up the quarter. But by then it was too late. I had already fallen so far behind in my classes that even studying through every weekend wasn't enough to bring my grades over a C average. At the end of the quarter I lost my scholarship. I dropped out and moved back home.

Five years later, I finally did graduate, not from Stanford, but from San Jose State. That I got my degree from a state school rather than an expensive private college didn't at all diminish the joy in my brother's eyes when he met me at the foot of the stage moments after I took my diploma in hand.

"Hold onto this for me," I said, giving it to him. "You know how disorganized I am. I'll just end up throwing it out by accident one of these days."

It wasn't until six months later, after I had been working full-time in my first office job, that I was finally able to pay Megan back the money she'd lent me. But when I called her in New York, where she was finishing her second year of law school at Cornell, she wouldn't hear of it. "Do something good with it," she said. "Just make sure you get out here soon. I'm tired of flying west every six months just to visit you."

After I hung up the phone, I thought for a while about all we had been through, marveled at how in just three months at Stanford so much had changed for me. Then I sat down at my desk to check over the assignments my brother had asked me to review for him for the classes he was taking in order to pass his high-school equivalency exam. It is a ritual I have come to repeat every night, with the care I rarely ever gave my own work when I was in school. I do it in the privacy of my den office, long after Martín, who now lives with me, has fallen into a deep, peaceful sleep.

About
The Chicano/Latino
Literary Prize

THE CHICANO/LATINO LITERARY PRIZE was first awarded by the Department of Spanish and Portuguese at the University of California, Irvine during the 1974-1975 academic year. In the quarter-century that has followed, this annual competition has clearly demonstrated the wealth and vibrancy of Hispanic creative writing to be found in the United States. Among the prize winners have been—to name a few among many—such accomplished authors as Lucha Corpi, Graciela Limón, Cherrie Moraga, Carlos Morton, Gary Soto, and Helena María Viramontes. Specific literary forms are singled out for attention each year on a rotating basis, including the novel, the short-story collection, drama, and poetry; and first-, second-, and third-place prizes are awarded. For more information on the Chicano/Latino Literary Prize, please contact:

Contest Coordinator
Chicano/Latino Literary Contest
Department of Spanish and Portugese
University of California, Irvine
Irvine, California 92697